Monica turr

but her feet got twisted in the long length of her robe and sent her body careening toward him as she tripped.

Reacting swiftly, Gabe reached to wrap his arm around her waist and brace her body against him to prevent her fall. Their faces were just precious inches apart. He squinted when her eyes dropped to his mouth. That evoked a small gasp from him as he allowed his eyes to scan her face before locking with hers.

He wondered what it felt like for her. Was her heart pounding? Her pulse sprinting? Was she aroused? Did she feel that pull of desire?

With a tiny lick of her lips that was nearly his undoing, Monica raised her chin.

"Monica?" he asked, his voice deep but soft as he sought clarity even as he felt heady with desire.

"Kiss me," she whispered against his lips with hunger.

Dear Reader,

Welcome to a sexy new romance read. For those who know me—hello again. For the first timers—nice to meet you! I may be new to Desire's line of wonderful books, but I am not new to romance. I like to think my books are "sexy, funny and oh so real," and *One Night with Cinderella* fits the bill. The love story of Gabe and Monica is just as magical as the title implies. I hope you all enjoy the ride as one wild and passionate night awakens feelings in this sexy mogul chef and the family's shy housekeeper—who gains her voice with a surprise multimillion-dollar inheritance!

Looking for chemistry that leaps off the pages, humor that makes you smile or laugh out loud, warmth that makes you believe in love, and enough family secrets and drama to keep you flipping the pages? Then pour a drink, find a quiet corner and get into this romance, which I hope will leave you absolutely breathless.

Isn't romance grand?

Best,

N.

NIOBIA BRYANT

ONE NIGHT WITH CINDERELLA

HARLEQUIN
DESIRE

HARLEQUIN®
DESIRE™

Recycling programs for this product may not exist in your area.

ISBN-13: 978-1-335-23273-1

One Night with Cinderella

Copyright © 2021 by Niobia Bryant

This edition published by arrangement with Harlequin Books S.A.

For questions and comments about the quality of this book, please contact us at CustomerService@Harlequin.com.

Harlequin Enterprises ULC
22 Adelaide St. West, 40th Floor
Toronto, Ontario M5H 4E3, Canada
www.Harlequin.com

Printed in U.S.A.

Niobia Bryant is the award-winning and nationally bestselling author of more than forty works of romance and mainstream commercial fiction. Twice she has won the RT Reviewers' Choice Best Book Award for African American/Multicultural Romance. Her books have appeared in *Ebony*, *Essence*, *New York Post*, *The Star-Ledger*, *Dallas Morning News* and many other national publications. One of her bestselling books was adapted to film.

Books by Niobia Bryant

Harlequin Desire

One Night with Cinderella

Harlequin Kimani

A Billionaire Affair
Tempting the Billionaire

Harlequin Kimani Arabesque

Count On This
You Never Know
Let's Do It Again
Can't Get Next to You

Visit the Author Profile page at Harlequin.com, or niobiabryant.com, for more titles.

You can also find Niobia Bryant on Facebook, along with other Harlequin Desire authors, at Facebook.com/harlequindesireauthors!

For all the romance readers who have supported
my career these last twenty-one years.
Cheers to a new romance!

One

"One day I hope I'm as rich as I look right now."

Monica Darby turned this way and that in the full-length, wood-framed mirror leaning against the wall of the spacious walk-in closet. The bright crimson of the couture gown she held in front of her body was so different from the dark tones she normally wore. With her free hand, she gathered her ponytail atop her head and sucked in her cheeks as she struck a dramatic model-like pose.

She felt like a little girl playing dress-up.

In the reflection, she caught sight of the price tag dangling from the sleeve. She checked it, not surprised to see it cost nearly a fourth of her annual salary. It was one of five extravagant garments delivered that morning. Each more glamorous and decadent than the last.

Monica imagined what it would be like to own such beautiful clothing, live in a luxurious home and jet all over the world at a whim.

Only in my dreams.

She reached up to hang the dress among the other expensive gowns, fearing being caught having a brief moment of folly into a lifestyle in which she lived on the fringe as the housekeeper to the powerful Cress family—a position she cherished because, in their home, she had found the stability she lacked growing up in foster care. With one last glance back at the closet to ensure it was pristine and in order, she turned and left the space, closing the French doors behind her.

Her sneaker-covered feet barely made any noise against the herringbone pattern of the polished hardwood floors as she crossed the suite to retrieve the caddie of her cleaning supplies. "Eight suites down and the kitchen to go," Monica said to herself before leaving the room and entering the spacious den that centered the top-floor hall of the five-story town house in the prominent and historic Lenox Hill section of Manhattan's Upper East Side.

The ten-thousand-square-foot home was quiet as she made her way to the elevator. She was the only in-house staff. The chef was out shopping, and all of the Cress family members were gone for the day. She had the peace she needed to clean without intrusion.

When the lift came to a stop, she opened the wrought-iron gate and stepped on, pulling the rolling caddie behind her before pressing the button for the finished basement level, where the items not sent out for dry cleaning were awaiting laundering. Her bedroom was located there, as well.

Ding.

She frowned when the elevator slowed. She thought she was alone and clearly, she was wrong. Her eyes widened as it came to a stop on the fourth floor and she was looking through the bronzed wrought iron at Gabriel Cress, known to everyone as Gabe. The middle son of Phillip and Nicolette Cress was busy looking down at his iPhone. She licked her lips as she stepped back until her spine was pressed to the wall and lowered her head. Her heart raced and thundered inside her chest so crazily that she feared he would hear it.

He looked up briefly and nodded his head at seeing her. "Mornin'," he said, his voice deep and obligatory, as the wrought-iron gate squealed a bit at being opened.

Her pulse pounded. "Good morning, Mr. Cress," she said, her voice soft as she kept her eyes on the tip of the sensible black sneakers she wore.

This gorgeous man made her so *very* nervous.

Monica wished she could fold herself into a much smaller version or fade into the woodwork lining the walls. Not that it mattered. She chanced a fleeting look up. He stood off to the side in front of her with his attention still focused on the screen of his phone. He barely noticed her. She was used to that. Men such as Gabe Cress—strong, handsome, sexy, wealthy and confident—were drawn to women so very unlike

Monica the Housekeeper, with her all-black uniform and face free of makeup.

She let her eyes study his profile.

He was a handsome man with a strong resemblance to the actor Jesse Williams. Shortbread complexion. Grayish-blue eyes. Square jaw and high cheekbones. Soft mouth. Short haircut with just the shadow of a beard. Tall—over six feet—with an athletic frame that was well defined and perfectly dressed in a crisp navy shirt tucked into dark denims with a cognac belt and polished handmade shoes. It was his signature outfit, seemingly simple but still stylish and tailored.

It had been five years since she was hired by his mother, Nicolette, but she still had not got used to him. Or the scent of his cologne. The warm and spicy scent reached her without being loud and cloying. It made her tingle.

All of the five Cress sons were handsome, but it was only Gabe that sent her into a tizzy. Only him.

Grab a hold of yourself, Monica.

For her, being enclosed with him in the elevator was like standing in the open doorway of a plane before spreading her arms wide and leaping to feel that quick shift from nervous anticipation to the sweet glory of free-falling through the air.

He was overwhelming without even trying to be so.

The elevator slid to a smooth stop and he slipped his phone into the back pocket of his denims before opening the gate. He offered her a brisk, congenial nod as he strode away.

She released the breath she must have been holding,

finding it shaky as she closed her eyes and lightly bit down on her bottom lip as she awaited recovery. She was used to it. The man just did *it* for her. She couldn't explain it. It was quite unfamiliar. And she didn't even want to want him.

But there *it* was.

That spark.

"Gabe and Monica sitting in a tree. He's I-G-N-O-R-I-N-G me," she said dryly before allowing herself a self-deprecating little chuckle as the elevator continued its descent to the basement.

Not that she wanted the attention of him or any other man. As far as she was concerned, love spelled nothing but a bunch of trouble.

She enjoyed her life of solitude. She spent her days keeping the family's home organized and tidy before retiring to her maid quarters and enjoying a night of television or reading. She felt safe from the disappointment and hurt she'd felt all her life growing up in the foster care system, never feeling at home or fitting in…and wondering why her parents didn't want her for themselves.

Monica pushed away the all-too-familiar pain she felt at being abandoned, thankful time had dulled it to just an ache. She shook her head a little as she stepped off the elevator into the basement, moving past the wine cellar, storage room and utility closet—every area grander than the next. She refused to give her unknown parents that type of power over her life—just as she had the numerous social workers, case managers and foster families she encountered as she was shifted from various group homes and foster families throughout her childhood.

She did not emotionally invest in anyone.

Love had let her down one time too many.

Look how my last relationship turned out.

As she rolled the caddie into the closet where she kept some of her cleaning supplies, she paused with her hand on the door. Remembering him.

James.

She rolled her eyes and shook her head, wishing life had rewind and delete buttons.

Once she aged out of the system at eighteen when the government deemed her an adult, Monica had been lucky enough to attend a community college and acquire a studio apartment, relying on school grants, loans and a part-time job to pay her way. Times had been tough and lean. Never had she felt so afraid that she wouldn't be able to make it on her own but also so determined to enjoy her freedom. She had been a student there for two years when she'd met and fallen in love with James Gilligan, a handsome travel photographer who convinced her to drop out of college and go RVing across the country with him as he documented his adventures on his popular blog. Leaving school had been a huge choice, but she felt she finally had someone who loved her and hadn't dared to risk losing him. Their travels and nomadic lifestyle lasted five years, filled with fun and spontaneity, until they traveled back to New York for a brief visit and she awakened one morning to discover he had left her behind to search for his next quest without her.

Monica grunted at her foolishness, hating how heartache and betrayal had left such an imprint. It'd been five years since she'd had to gather her wits, put aside her tears and make a new plan for her life. The advertisement for an in-house staff position had seemed like an answer to her prayers, providing a job and a place to stay. She applied and then thankfully accepted the position when it was offered.

Once she had work to focus on, she resolved to never give someone the chance to hurt her and leave her behind again.

Like her parents.

Like so many foster parents.

Like James.

Monica sighed as that poignant ache of bitter disappointment radiated across her chest. His treachery still affected her. She hated that so much.

She closed the door to the supply closet and moved over to open the door to the stylish and brightly lit laundry room, where she loaded two high-capacity washers with bed linen that she changed every day. While the machines quietly went to work, she walked to the other end of the basement to her quarters. It was a lovely little suite comprised of a bedroom, adjoining bathroom and small sitting area. She'd decorated the area in shades of yellow to give it more warmth, make it feel a little bit like her own, since it was the longest she'd ever been in one residence.

She pulled a small stack of envelopes from the front pocket of her apron to put on the side table near the recliner to sort through later. The family's mail was left on an ostrich leather tray in the foyer, as was customary. Leaving her room, she closed the door and retraced her steps until she reached the stairs to make her way up to the modern and brightly lit kitchen on the first level. The space, with its dark wood against light walls, chrome appliances and bronzed fixtures, was as beautifully designed as the rest of the town house.

The family's chef, Jillian Rossi, was out doing her daily shopping, and Monica always used that time to clean the kitchen from what little mess was left over from the family's breakfast dishes. Before loading the dishwasher, she opened it to find the high-end cutlery she knew belonged to Jillian from the initials engraved on the handles. She spotted the chef's leather carry case on the granite counter and retrieved it, undid the clasp and unrolled it.

A handwritten note was inside.

"'The taste of you still lingers on my tongue,'" she read aloud.

Well, well, well, Jillian...

Monica furrowed her brow as she rolled the carry case back as it had been, wishing she'd never seen the note—or the embossed gold Cress, INC. logo at the top. In such a large, affluent family, whose members chose to do business *and* live together, secrets weren't scarce. She'd seen and heard plenty in her five years. Hidden safes. Vices. Stubborn grudges. Business deals. Promises made. Promises broken. Even two of the brothers unknowingly dating the same sexy socialite. Discovering that one of the Cress men was enjoying a secret tryst with Jillian the Chef—complete with a handwritten note in this day and age—was light work in comparison.

It was none of her business, but Monica couldn't help but wonder which one.

Phillip Jr.? Or Sean? Cole? Maybe Lucas?

She winced as she pictured Gabe passionately kissing Jillian. She had no right to the jealousy warming her stomach. If Gabe and Jillian were secret lovers then it was no concern of hers.

Right?

Right.

Still, at that moment, it was feeling easier said than done.

Gabe stroked his chin as he stared at the waterfall fountain at the end of the paved garden area. Winter was just truly beginning to break and the air was crisp and refreshing instead of biting and chilly. He sat at the long concrete table beneath the arched framework that covered the full thirty-two-foot length of the area with the leaves of bamboo trees offering the family privacy and shade when they were outdoors. The sounds of New York on the adjacent busy Lexington Avenue reached him, but it was vague background noise as he focused instead on his thoughts.

Serving as the president of the restaurant division of Cress, INC. made him responsible for making decisions that produced results. Phillip Cress Sr., his stalwart father and the company's chief executive officer, expected nothing less and made that fact clear with all of his sons. Gabe was a strong-willed man with his own vision and ideas, but he had little patience. He was finding it tiresome proving himself worthy to a domineering father who expected nothing but blind allegiance.

Gabe wished his father knew his loyalty to his family existed because he loved his parents and his brothers above all and would do anything to see them happy. Making sacrifices wasn't new. Gabe had always tried so very hard to be unproblematic for his parents. With five rowdy boys and a busy professional life that had led to stellar careers, his parents hadn't needed an extra hassle. Another child to discipline. Another child to worry about. It had become his custom to keep his head tucked down, stick to himself and never disappoint the parents he admired. The accomplishments of his parents could not be overlooked or disrespected.

Phillip Cress Sr. and Nicolette Lavoie-Cress loved cooking second only to their five sons. Over the past fifty years they had established themselves as acclaimed and well-respected chefs, won Michelin stars and James Beard Awards, established many successful restaurants, and written more than two dozen bestselling cookbooks and culinary guides. As they began to slow down, the couple increasingly focused on growing the powerful culinary empire of Cress, INC. and diversifying their business to nationally syndicated cooking shows, cookware, online magazines, an accredited cooking school, which Nicolette operated, and a nonprofit foundation.

The couple had also passed their love of cooking on to their sons, who were all acclaimed chefs in their own right. Each son also played a role in the business. Gabe headed up the restaurant division. His oldest brother, Phillip Jr., ran the nonprofit, the Cress Family Foundation. Sean supervised the syndicated cooking shows. Cole oversaw the online magazines and websites. And their baby brother, Lucas, had just been appointed head of the cookware line.

But now Phillip Sr. was looking to one of them to groom as his successor to the Cress, INC. throne, and each of the Cress sons wanted the coveted prize of leading the family business into the future. And to have their father, who they all respected, give such a nod would be the ultimate testament and acknowledgment of their abilities. Still, it made for competitiveness and minor flare-ups among the brothers, which Gabe was finding tiresome. They had always been raised to be loving and loyal to one another. With each passing day, sadly, he saw less of that allegiance.

At times working and living together was a handful. Thus, his day of working from home and not at their corporate offices in Midtown Manhattan. He needed a breather. Of everyone in the family, he hated useless confrontations and arguing the most. He found it tedious.

His stomach grumbled, and he picked up his phone from where it sat atop his open files on the table. It was nearing lunch and he had skipped breakfast. Rising, he slid his phone in the front pocket of his tailored shirt, moved down the length of the garden and opened the sliding door of the glass wall of the dining room.

Across the dining room he spotted their housekeeper, Monica, closing the dishwasher and pressing the buttons to turn it on before she briskly walked over to the pantry. He hadn't seen her moving about the kitchen when he was in the garden, but he wasn't surprised. She was a great housekeeper, who they all trusted with their home and possessions, but she also made sure not to intrude on their lives. She barely spoke and rarely made eye contact. She was...skittish.

This morning in the elevator, if she had pressed her body back against the wall any more, she could have melded with it. It's why he hadn't bothered with much conversation. He hadn't been sure she wouldn't jump out of her own skin if he said too much.

Five years, and he doubted he'd spoken more than a dozen words to her in all that time.

Reaching the kitchen, Gabe opened the Sub-Zero to study the many contents for something to feed his hunger. He was almost tempted to prepare his own favorite dish of homemade ravioli stuffed with a mixture of wild mushroom, ricotta and parmesan cheese served in a bisque. Almost. It had been nearly three years since he departed his role as the head chef of the Midtown Manhattan CRESS restaurant. Cress, INC. came first. Gabe hardly ever cooked that much anymore. In fact, no one in the family did. There wasn't time. Thus, the need for a family of chefs to have a chef on staff to cook for them.

With the release of a deep breath he acknowledged how much he missed being a chef. That alone was the clearest example of his loyalty to his family and his desire to help his parents further their dreams of a culinary empire.

"Oh. Sorry."

He closed the door a bit and looked over his shoulder at Monica, standing in the entry to the pantry. Her eyes were wide with surprise before she looked down at the cleaning supplies she held in her hands.

"Jillian's not here, Mr. Cress," she said, her words rushed. Awkward.

He frowned. "Jillian? Do I need her permission to enter the kitchen?" he asked sternly, giving her an odd look before turning back to the fridge and removing a container of leftover ginger-lime carrots and another of seared scallops.

"No…no. Of course not. I just thought you were looking for her. Just…never mind," she said, shaking her head as she set the supplies on the counter and began walking out of the room.

Annoyance sparked in him. *This is ridiculous.*

"Have I done something to offend you or make you so uneasy around me?" he asked, feeling as if she saw him as a wolf about to jump on his prey.

Of that, she shouldn't worry. This shy and reserved woman unable to look him in the eye was hardly his type. He was tempted by fire and confident sex appeal. She appeared afraid of her own shadow.

Monica whirled, her face filled with her surprise. "Of course not, Mr. Cress," she insisted.

Gabe was surprised by the sudden knot in his gut as he eyed the rare show of emotion she displayed. The first he'd seen in five years. It opened her face. Brought life and light to it. And interest. For the first time, he noticed she was pretty. If by instinct his eyes quickly took in all of her. A man studying a woman.

She favored Zoe Saldana. Medium brown complexion. Long dark brown hair pulled into a loose ponytail that emphasized her high cheekbones and doe-shaped eyes with long lashes. Beneath her black T-shirt and pants, he could tell she was tall and slender but curvy. He even found the flat mole near the corner of her left eye intriguing.

He wondered just what other emotion she hid beneath the surface. Passion? Desire? Pleasure? Satisfaction?

How would her face be transformed during her climax? Dazed eyes? Gaped mouth?

The thought of that caused his heart to skip a beat, as temptation rose with a quickness.

Easy, Gabe. Easy.

"I just wanted to make sure I've never done anything to make you uncomfortable with me," he said, setting aside the allure of a subdued woman with hints of fire beneath the surface—a taste in women he had never known himself to have before.

She looked at him and visibly swallowed over a lump in her throat. "No. Never," she assured him, her voice soft.

No. Not soft. Husky. Throaty.

Well, well, well. Who knew?

"I don't want to interrupt your schedule," Gabe said, crossing the kitchen to retrieve a plate from the glass-paned cabinet she stood beside. "I'm just getting some lunch because I'm working from home today."

She stepped back from his sudden nearness.

He frowned a bit as he looked down at her. Their eyes met for a brief moment before she looked away. She had to be close to his age of thirty-two, so her nervousness piqued his curiosity. "Monica," he said, his voice low.

She looked up at him. "Sir?" she said, wringing her hands together in front of her.

Oh.

Her truth was in the depths of her doe-shaped eyes.

Gabe was a man quite familiar with women. As a chef he was a connoisseur of wine, needing the right accoutrement to the food he created. His experience with women reached the same expert level. Standing before him was a woman made nervous because she liked him. Was aware of him. Desired him.

Of *that* he was sure.

His body warmed over at the thought of her interest. He cleared his throat and moved back across the kitchen to plate his food before warming it in the microwave.

Bzzzzzz.

He reached for his vibrating phone and checked the caller ID. It was an old acquaintance calling. Felicity. He thought of the tall and shapely beauty with big eyes, lips and thighs, but didn't answer the call. It had been weeks since they'd spent time together, and he wasn't interested in striking up a new round of their on-again, off-again dalliance. She'd wanted nothing more than access to his upscale lifestyle, and he'd been satisfied with beautiful arm candy who was very eager to do nothing more than keep a smile on his face. Her first not-so-subtle hint of marriage had cooled his ardor.

Gabe was as adamant about his success in business as he was about avoiding a serious relationship. His romantic history had proven he was unable to balance the expectations of love and the duties of his career without someone suffering, so he chose the latter, enjoying the prestige, the challenge and the admiration of a father who, like himself, expected nothing but the very best.

Felicity had unknowingly served as a reminder of the sophisticated and sexy women he favored. Very unlike Monica.

Not that it mattered. She was a part of the family staff and off-limits.

He looked over to where she had stood and wasn't surprised to find the spot now empty.

That's for the best.

The last thing he wanted was to encourage her and then have her be disappointed when nothing came of her crush. He was more interested in her skill at organizing and cleaning his private bedroom suite than having her in it beneath him on his bed as he sated her desire.

Our *desire*, he admitted to himself.

Had things been different—time and place—and had she had a little more flash and sass about her, Gabe knew he would've gladly satisfied the craving he saw in her eyes.

Two

One week later

Gabe loosened his black silk tuxedo bow tie, leaving it to hang beneath the collar of his black shirt as he leaned in the doorway of the newest CRESS restaurant. It was the tenth such venture of Cress, INC., and as the president of its restaurant division, this was a personal celebration. He'd overseen every stage of its creation from its high-end modern design to its menu of French cuisine, and the selection of the head chef and staff.

His entire family was gathered in one of the four private rooms of CRESS X, celebrating its grand opening. The champagne had been drunk. The meal savored. The compliments shared, along with some business talk about current plans for the Cress, INC. empire.

He took a sip of vintage champagne as he looked over the rim of the crystal flute at his brothers.

Phillip Jr., the eldest son, pressed a warm kiss to the neck of his wife, Raquel, as she rubbed the back of their very sleepy toddler, Collette, stretched across their laps. Whatever he whispered in her ear brought a slow smile to her face.

Gabe could only imagine, and that made him chuckle into his glass.

His next eldest brother, Sean, moved about the room with his brandy snifter in hand, in full-charm mode. He hosted several culinary shows produced by Cress, INC., ran with high-profile celebrities and had snagged a spot as one of *People*'s Top Ten Sexiest Chefs last year. Thankfully his smile and culinary skills were as big as his ego.

His two youngest brothers, Cole and Lucas, both glanced over at a pretty server moving around the table, touching up everyone's drinks, before they shared a wolfish smile that revealed they both appreciated her appeal, even though they didn't dare to act upon it. Although Gabe wouldn't put it past Cole to defy the rule and enjoy a night in her bed. He seemed to love going left just because everyone else went right.

Lucas was the youngest Cress son and, hands down, his parents' favorite. They all knew it and accepted it. These days it wasn't clear from his chiseled frame that he used to carry an extra fifty pounds from his mother's indulgence.

Everyone had long since been assigned a role. Phil, the responsible one. Sean, the star. Cole, the rebel, and

Lucas, the fave. Gabe knew he was the good one. The nonproblematic middle child.

He flexed his shoulders and took another deep swig of his drink.

Ding-ding-ding.

The blend of voices and cutlery hitting plates silenced as everyone turned their attention to his father, just having stood and now tapping a fork against his flute. Gabe eyed the tall solid dark-skinned man with broad features and a bright smile.

"We've shared forty years together, my love," Phillip Sr. began, his English accent thick and his eyes locked on his wife, Nicolette, an olive-skinned beauty whose silvery locks held a hint of her past blond color. "Together we have accomplished so much and we did it with love. Of each other. Of our family. Of enjoying life. Of food."

Gabe smiled as his mother reached to slide her hand into his father's and softly stroke his palm with her thumb.

"And we passed that love on to our children—our sons. *Five,*" he stressed, patting his chest in pride.

The room filled with chuckles.

From the time they were small, the Cress boys had learned firsthand about food and the best way to cook it. To appreciate its nuances and how varying techniques brought out different results—all delicious. Each of them had trained in their parents' restaurants and attended culinary school, then traveled different paths to become chefs. All were skilled culinary experts with a love of food that their parents had passed to them through their genes and home training.

"Tonight, we celebrate yet another success for Cress, INC.," Phillip said, eyeing his adult children. "An empire that is the greatest manifestation of our two greatest loves. Food and family."

Nicolette rose to stand beside her husband. *"À la nourriture. À la vie. À l'amour."*

His mother's favorite saying in her native French tongue. To food. To life. To love.

It was painted on the wall above all of her stoves—personal and professional—on the base of every pan in the Cress line of cookware, in the watermark of every letter from the various editors of their culinary magazines. It was also branded on all their online presences and the saying at the end of the cooking shows produced by Cress, INC.'s television division.

"À la nourriture. À la vie. À l'amour," they all repeated in unison as they raised their flutes in toast.

Phillip Sr. and Nicolette shared a kiss and then a few more until they stopped with a reluctance that was clear. He took her hand in his and led her to the small area in the middle of the room, designed in shades of linen and bronze, before pulling her close to him to dance as he softly sang a French love song in her ear.

Gabe looked at them. He was single and mingling to his heart's content without a thought of the lasting love his parents shared. Life had long since proven to him that he was a failure at balancing love and his ambition.

He stopped the pretty server with a polite and distant smile before setting his empty flute on the tray she held. "Thank you," he said, unbuttoning the single button of his tailored black tuxedo jacket before turning to leave the room unnoticed.

For him, the night and the celebrating were over.

He made his way down the hall and then through the front of the house, barely taking note of the contemporary design, high ceilings and lush decor as he left the Tribeca restaurant and made his way to his waiting SUV. The driver left his seat and came around the front of the polished black vehicle to hold the rear passenger door for him.

Gabe thanked him with a nod and relaxed against the plush leather as soon as he'd folded his body onto the seat. The combination of champagne and the premium cuts of perfectly marbled and aged Miyazaki A5 Wagyu strip steak had been delicious but tiring. He was ready for a little solitude and self-reflection before the family returned from the restaurant and the festivities most likely continued.

Upon reaching the town house, under the cloak of darkness broken up by towering streetlamps, Gabe jogged up the stately steps and pressed his thumb to the biometric sensor to unlock the wrought-iron door and enter the marbled foyer. The length of the entire first floor was dimly lit with small pockets of light, breaking the darkness of night. With long strides he made his way across the wood floors of the living room through to the spacious chef's kitchen.

On top of the island counter awaited a case of champagne and a dozen flutes.

Whistling, he grabbed a bottle and a flute to carry

over to the elevator in the corner. He paused as he stepped on the lift and eyed the rear wall. He remembered that day when he'd walked in and barely noticed Monica standing there with her back pressed against it, as if trying to blend into it. A day like so many others. What was different was later that day, in the kitchen, he saw her—really saw her—for the first time.

And he had liked what he'd seen.

Still do.

He frowned, turning as he held the bottle and glass between the fingers of one hand and pressed the illuminated button for the rooftop with the other. The elevator gently shifted upward as he remembered the look of desire in her eyes and how his heart had raced at the awareness that quiet, reliable Monica had a hidden desire for him.

The thought of her made his gut clench.

Her beauty was subtle. Quiet. But once recognized? Not to be denied.

He released a breath and shifted back and forth in his stance.

What was most important about Monica Darby was her aptitude at her job as their housekeeper. How she kept her head tucked down and completed her tasks without disturbing their lives or breaking their trust in her. Many times his mother had raved that she was integral to their busy lives, even going above and beyond what was asked. The house ran like a well-oiled machine because of her quietly completed tasks.

That mattered more than her doe-shaped eyes, heated by the fire of desire.

Ding.

The elevator slowed to a stop. With his free hand he opened the gate and stepped out onto the rooftop terrace that spanned the twenty-two-foot width of the building. The air was calm, not too hot, and the sounds of the city echoed as he moved past the open seating area and around the glasshouse.

At the sight of Monica leaning against the wrought-iron railing, looking over at Central Park, he paused. A spring wind blew and caused the hem of her floor-length cotton robe to lift a bit. Her hair was loose down her back. There was a hint of a smile at her lips, and the moonlight cast a sweet glow upon her profile as the fairy lights adorning the pergola seemed to twinkle behind her.

It was a little endearing and magical.

Like one of those romance movies his sister-in-law, Raquel, loved to watch.

Monica looked toward him just as he was about to turn, leaving her to her solitude.

"Oh, I'm sorry, Mr. Cress," she said, shifting to face him. "I thought the family was out for the night."

Her robe and the high neck of the gown she wore beneath it was all very prim and proper. Very sedate. Very reserved. Very Monica.

"They are. I'm not. Well, not anymore," he said, holding up the bottle and flute. "Wanted to enjoy a moment alone before everyone got back."

She nodded in understanding. "I'll leave you to it," she said, tucking her hair behind her right ear as she walked toward him.

"We launched our newest restaurant, CRESS X, tonight," he said, surprised at the need to fill the silence.

Monica glanced up at him with an impish look. "I know," she said. "Congratulations."

Of course she knew. He doubted there was much she didn't know about everyone in the family. Thus the nondisclosure agreement she was required to sign when she was first hired.

There was a sudden squeal of car tires from down below.

They both quickly moved to the railing to look at the street. A bright red sports car swerved to the right of a blue convertible before racing away.

"The aftermath of a near collision," Gabe said, glancing over at her, standing beside him.

"Hopefully everyone will get home safe," she said.

Gabe took in her high cheekbones, the soft roundness of her jaw and the tilt of her chin. The scent of something subtle but sweet surrounded her. He forced his eyes away from her and cleared his throat. "Hopefully," he agreed as he poured a small amount of champagne into the flute.

"I'll leave you to celebrate," Monica said.

With a polite nod, Gabe took a sip of his drink and set the bottle on the roof at his feet, trying to ignore he was so aware of her. Her scent. Her beauty. Even the gentle night winds shifting her hair back from her face. Distance was best. Over the last week he had fought to do just that to help his sudden awareness of her ebb. Ever since the veil to *their* desire had been removed, it had been hard to ignore.

She turned to leave but moments later a yelp escaped her as her feet got twisted in the long length of her robe and sent her body careening toward him as she tripped.

Reacting swiftly, he reached to wrap his arm around her waist and brace her body up against his to prevent her fall. He let the hand holding his flute drop to his side. Their faces were just precious inches apart. When her eyes dropped to his mouth, he released a small gasp. His eyes scanned her face before locking with hers.

He knew just fractions of a second had passed, but right then, with her in his arms and their eyes locked, it felt like an eternity. He wondered what it felt like for her. Was her heart pounding? Her pulse sprinting? Was she aroused? Did she feel that pull of desire?

He did.

With a tiny lick of her lips that was nearly his undoing, Monica raised her chin and kissed him. It was soft and sweet. And an invitation.

"Monica?" he asked, heady with desire but his voice deep and soft as he sought clarity.

"Kiss me," she whispered against his lips, hunger in her voice.

"Shit," Gabe swore before he gave in to the temptation of her and dipped his head to press his mouth down upon hers.

And it was just a second more before her lips and her body softened against him as she opened her mouth and welcomed him with a heated gasp that seemed to echo around them. The first touch of his tongue to hers sent a jolt through his body, and he clenched her closer to him as her hands snaked up his arms and then his shoulders before clutching the lapels of his tux in her fists. He assumed she was holding on while giving in to a passion that was irresistible.

Monica was lost in it all. Blissfully.

The taste and feel of his mouth were everything she ever imagined.

Ever dreamed.

Ever longed for.

She was lost in a heady mix of surprise and excitement as she raised slightly trembling hands to stroke the back of his head. A moan from deep within her escaped. His grunt quickly followed. Somewhere in the heat of it all, she heard the flute crash against the roof as he released his hold on the drink to drag his hand up the back of her thighs.

He tasted her lips before pressing heated kisses down to her throat where she felt him deeply inhale her scent before suckling that little dip above her clavicle. She gasped and cried out as she flung her head back giving him more of her neck to taste. She clung to him, lifting and bending her leg to the side of his solid body and being rewarded by his hand gripping her buttocks through the cotton, feeling the heat of his touch.

"Gabe," she whispered into the air, saying his first name aloud for the first time ever.

And what a time to do so.

When she'd noticed him standing there, looking so sharp and handsome in his black tuxedo with a bottle of champagne in his hand, he'd seemed to have stepped straight off the pages of a high-fashion magazine or some cologne ad. With his shirt open at the neck and his tie undone, she'd felt pushed over the edge of reason, no matter how well she'd covered it. Just tempting. Strong, dark and sexy. Devastatingly so.

Her heart had pounded with both surprise and a desire that took her breath away.

And now he was kissing her. And touching her. And pressing her body against his.

Am I dreaming?

Her mouth sought his and he accepted her boldness when she offered him her tongue. With a grunt of pleasure, he sucked the tip into his mouth. Deeply. And then did it again. And again. She trembled. Her pulse raced and she ached deep inside her womanhood.

Don't wake me up.

Monica pressed her hands to the sides of his face, enjoying the feel of his shadow against her palms as she gently played with his earlobes and the soft skin just behind them. She felt the slight tremble of his body and knew she had happened upon his hot spot. Maybe one of many.

Against her thigh she felt the length of his hardness.

Breaking their kiss, she leaned back just a bit to look at him as she panted.

Their eyes locked and something happened between them. A current. A spark. A vibe. She felt it and shivered.

This was desire, and in it, they were equal.

"Monica?" he whispered into the small break between them.

It had been so long since she'd given in to pure carnal pleasure, but she couldn't remember ever feeling the thrill *his* touch brought her. Her entire body felt electrified. He was seeking approval to give her even *more* pleasure. When in her entire life had *more* ever been an option? After a lifetime of so many disappointments. So many dreams she never dared to give hope to. How could she deny herself *this*?

"Yes," she acquiesced, giving both him and herself permission.

Gabe swung her up into his arms and took long strides to reach the flower-covered pergola. There, beneath its cover, he pressed her down onto one of the round, double chaise longues, and the thick cushion welcomed her. He removed his jacket and flung away his bow tie. The shirt clung to the hard definitions of his body.

He got sexier?

Monica leaned against the pillows as the fleshy bud between her legs swelled to life. She watched him remove a condom packet from his wallet before undressing as she slowly untied the belt of her robe and opened it to fall at her sides. Her trembling hand paused at the top button of her nightgown as she took in the first sight of Gabe Cress—*the* Gabe Cress—standing before her gloriously naked.

Oh. My.

He was sculpted. Plain and simple. But then not simple at all, because the all of him was everything. Broad shoulders, narrow waist, eight-pack abs and strong thighs. The hair on his chest lay flat before narrowing to an arrow down the jagged middle line of his abs and connecting with the curly dark bush that surrounded the base of his smooth, thick and long hardness. It curved away from his body in a darker complexion than the rest of his light brown skin. Like milk chocolate. Decadent.

Gabe massaged the length of his inches before covering his hardness with their latex protection. He bent his body to crawl up the chaise. She hitched her matronly floral-print gown up her thighs as she opened her legs to him. She assumed he was going to press his body down upon hers, but instead he reached to undo each tiny pearl button running down the front of her gown. Somehow each one being undone seemed to send a jolt through her as more and more of her naked body was exposed to his. And when he reached the last one and flung the gown open, she arched her back and released a hot gasp as the spring wind floated across her body and hardened her nipples even more.

Gabe stroked and massaged her inner thighs before lying flat and then giving her a heated look as he lowered his head.

He couldn't. He wouldn't.

But he did.

The first feel of his clever tongue stroking against her bud was her undoing. Monica cried out and reached to grip the sides of his face as she rotated her hips while he sucked the all-too-sensitive bud into his mouth. As he pleasured her, she wished she had followed her instinct and done the same to him. Just imagining the feel of his hardness against her lips and her tongue as he tasted of her in the most intimate fashion, she felt breathless. She was lost in her passion but finding a piece of herself that she had locked away in her loneliness over the last five years.

It was a wonderful hello to her femininity. Her sexuality. Her being.

An awakening.

"Gabe, Gabe, Gabe," she gasped into the night air as she clutched at the pillows with her nails and dug in for control as she felt herself spiraling into an explosive climax that made her entire body feel so raw and exposed. So alive. In the best way. Ever.

Just as she was on the brink, Gabe quickly shifted his body atop hers and probed her wet and quivering core with the tip of his hard inches. She tilted her chin up and licked at his mouth as their eyes met. "Just this once," she said.

"Just once," he agreed with a nod, his eyes so dark and intense in his handsome face. "Then I better make it damn good."

"Please," she begged, wrapping her legs and arms around his body almost desperately as he used his hips to fill her with one swift thrust.

They cried out roughly.

They were united.

Connected.

Monica closed her eyes as she winced at the feel of him so tightly sheathed by her core. Every pulse of his dick seemed to pound against her walls. She knew he was fighting for control. Trying his best not to climax. She was glad her own peak waned off. For now.

She wasn't ready for their wild night atop the roof of the beautiful Victorian town house to end.

"Look at me."

She did as he bid.

Their eyes stayed locked on one another—lost in each other—as he began to stroke inside her. She felt it. From base to tip. Hardness. Thickness. Heat. Over and over again.

Feeling emboldened and lost in the carnal pleasure, she matched each thrust with a slow wind of her hips that tightened her walls down upon his shaft.

He pursed his lips at the move and then swore.

She knew she pleased him and she smiled, tilting her head to the side, her mouth agape, as she continued to match his stare. He dipped his head to kiss her and she tasted herself. It thrilled her as she sucked his tongue into her mouth with a low purr.

Their eyes were still locked. It was intense. And heady. And powerful.

His strokes deepened and he sped up the pace. She gasped as her eyes widened, and she could do nothing but give in to his passionate onslaught as she broke their stare and buried her face against his neck to muffle her cries of pleasure. He slid his hand beneath her to grip her bottom. She looked over his shoulder at the up-and-down motion of his buttocks as he stroked away. His muscles clenched with each movement. A trickle of sweat coursed down his back and disappeared in the deep groove between his hard buttocks.

It was a glorious sight to see.

He lightly bit down on her shoulder as his body went stiff.

"What's wrong?" she whispered in between pants.

He replaced his teeth with a kiss. "I don't want this to end. Not yet," he said, his own breathing labored as he waited for his orgasm to recede.

"No. Don't. Not yet," she agreed, turning her head to the side to face his.

They shared a soft laugh as they looked at one another.

Monica stroked the side of his face and was surprised when he turned his head to kiss her palm. She gave him an inquisitive look at the tender move.

"You're beautiful," he admitted.

She made a face of disbelief. "No, you are," she said, stroking his buttock with her heel as she massaged his back with her fingertips.

He chuckled.

She tightened her walls against his hardness.

He stopped laughing and shifted his arm around her waist to hold her close before turning both their bodies so that she was atop him. She looked down into his silvery-blue eyes that seemed to blaze against his light brown complexion. Her gaze searched his face. Missing nothing. Not even the small scar on his chin that was barely hidden by the shadow of his beard.

Feeling bold and confident, she removed his arm from around her and slowly sat up straight as she drew her hands up his sides and across his chest to press against his pecs. She flipped her hair back over her shoulder to have a clear view of his face as she began to ride him. His eyes seemed to fill with wonder as he watched her move her body like a snake, her one hand held up in the air.

Gabe ran his hands up her thighs to her belly and up to cup a breast in each hand.

"Aaaaaaah," Monica cried out, letting her head fall back so that the tips of her hair tickled the top of her buttocks as he eased one hand up to press against her throat with his index finger near her mouth.

She turned her head to suck the tip into her mouth and was rewarded when she felt him get harder inside of her. The base of his inches stroked against her bud, fueling the slow and steady rise of yet another climax. She was anxious for it to explode.

She moaned with a wince of pure anticipation.

Gabe sat up to draw one taut brown nipple into his mouth as he gripped her hips to slam down as he thrust his own upward, sending his hardness against her fleshy bud with slight force. Again. And again. And again.

The combination of him licking her nipples and her swollen and aching bud being plucked like a chord was earth-shattering. She quickened her pace, back and forth on his length, as he matched her speed. "Yes," she sighed. "Yes."

"I'm with you," he moaned against her cleavage before moving to her other breast to suck and lick it as if starved.

"Yes!" she exclaimed, her throat dry from her panting and gasps of pleasure. Her entire body felt heated as she exploded with the first sweet wave of her release.

Gabe roared with his own release as he held her tightly and continued to taste her nipples.

Monica was lost as she rested the side of her face atop his head and bit down on her bottom lip as she succumbed to her climax and felt a wave of pure pleasure made all the more electric by Gabe free-falling into the abyss with her. Their rough cries filled the air, blending with the drone of late-night traffic as their sexual haze came to a shuddering end that left them both sweaty, panting and fighting for control of the rapid pounding of their hearts.

As he lay back and she shifted her body on top of him, her head on his hard chest, she marveled at what they'd shared. She wondered if he had experienced such pleasure, such invisibility of inhibitions and such electricity before. Because she hadn't. Not ever. And wondered if she would ever again.

Just this once.

That had been her request, and she knew it was for the best. Even as they lay in each other's arms weakened by their explosive climax, regret was settling in. She nibbled at her bottom lip as reality returned. Gabe Cress, as beautiful and sexy as he was, and having far surpassed her seductive dreams, was one of her employers. She couldn't afford to lose the job she loved nor did she want encounters like this to be a regular occurrence. It was all so typical of upstairs-downstairs relationships.

Tonight had been just for me, but no more.

She hated the insecurity she felt even as she lay in

his arms. "Just once," she reminded him in a soft whisper as she listened to the pace of his heart begin to slow.

He nodded, and for moments she didn't count, he continued to hold her before he pressed a kiss to the top of her wild hair and rose from the chaise. A goodbye to their rendezvous.

Three

Two weeks later

Monica wiped her sweaty brow with the back of her hand before she rose from her knees and dropped the large sponge into the bucket of sudsy water.

"Thank you," Raquel said from her seat on one of the two custom-made, light gray velvet sectionals in the sizable den centering the fifth floor of the town house, where there were three bedrooms, each with their own attached bathroom.

"No problem, Mrs. Cress," she said, picking up the bucket from atop the silk Persian carpet in the same shades of gray and steel blue as the stylish decor throughout the entire town house.

"Apologize to Miss Monica for your mess, Collette."

Moments after she heard Raquel's request to her and Phillip Jr.'s daughter, Collette, Monica felt a gentle tug on her pants leg. She turned and looked down at the precocious three-year-old with dimpled cheeks and bright yellow spectacles that made her all the more adorable.

"I'm sorry I spilled my milk, Miss Monica," she said.

"No worries, Colli," she said with a soft smile, using the child's pet name. "No worries at all."

With her absolution, the little girl went running back across the room to sit at her mother's feet where she'd been playing with her iPad.

Monica made a mental note to have the rug removed for professional cleaning. Once done dumping the bucket, she used the wrought-iron staircase running along the north side of the house to go back down to the fourth floor where she had been cleaning the bedroom suites before being summoned upstairs to attend to the spill.

She crossed the den that was the exact same design as the one upstairs, with the glass letting in so much spring light to shine against the hardwood floors and elaborate woodwork of the custom shelving and doors. She retrieved her cleaning caddie and pulled it behind her to Gabe's bedroom suite on the far end. Her steps faltered a bit. This was his sanctuary, and after their lovemaking, entering it felt all the more nerve-racking.

At the door she took a long breath and wet her lips before finally opening it and entering his spacious suite decorated in stylish shades of gray, from charcoal to smoke. Her eyes fell on his unmade king-size bed and she envisioned him lying there nude as he slept.

"Just once. Then I better make it damn good."

Closing her eyes, she shook her head to erase the hot thought and the memory of his words *that* night. Two weeks later and it was still scorched into her memory. She looked down at the goose bumps on her arms, brought on at the very thought of him.

Get it together, Mo.

She forged ahead, swiftly crossing the room to open gray suede curtains, exposing the glass wall that gave him a view of the city landscape in the distance. She used the leather ties to secure them back before moving over to the bed to take up the coverlet, the blanket folded across the foot and the crisp white cotton sheets. With them gathered in her arms and pressed against her chest, it was hard to ignore the scent of him rising from the bed linens.

Like a silly schoolgirl with a crush, she allowed herself to press her nose against the sheets for a deep inhale that took her back in time to that night.

"Oh. My apologies, Monica."

Frightened, she released a squeal and dropped the covers to the silk rug as she looked at Gabe, standing in the now open doorway of his en suite bathroom. Her eyes dipped to avoid his bare chest but then fell to the towel barely clinging to his hips. She gasped and turned from him, wishing the sound of her harsh breathing didn't echo so loudly in the air.

"Um. Sorry, Mr. Cress. I thought you were already

gone for the day," she said, moving quickly toward
the door.

"Monica. Wait. I didn't know you were here either,"
he called behind her in explanation.

"I'll wait outside," she said, her words rushing together with the same quick pace of her heart.

As soon as she closed the door, she stepped over to
press her back against the wall and looked up at the
tray ceiling with the brocade design, a nod to the Victorian era in which the home was first constructed.
So delicate and ornate, she thought, trying to focus
on anything but the sight of the plush towel wrapped
around Gabe.

Monica remembered that night on the roof so very
well.

She shook her head, now focusing her gaze outside
the glass to the swaying emerald leaves of the towering tree in the backyard. She and Gabe had fallen back
into their cordiality, but her awareness of him had not
been lessened by the coupling. If anything, it made
it all the worse. Simple touches—as she handed him
something or passed him in a hall—sent her pulse racing. Her dreams at night were consumed by him and
their passion.

In a perfect world—where she was not an employee
and had lineage and wealth of her own—she would
more than gladly have him as her lover. But that was
not her truth, and although it hurt her pride and stoked
insecurities, she knew that one night had been all Gabe
Cress would ever desire from his family's housekeeper.

So move on, Mo the Maid. Move on. There is noth-

*ing but heartache for you at the end of this road. Just
like before.*

She winced. Thinking of her ex, James, at a time
like this was insult on top of injury.

The door to Gabe's bedroom opened. She pushed
off the wall to stand tall, clasping her hands and past-
ing a blank expression on her face.

He exited.

And, of course, he looked handsome in a lightweight
tan suit that was perfectly tailored to his frame.

"Thank you, Monica," he said, his tone indicat-
ing nothing more than the cordiality one would give a
stranger. "Have a good day."

"You, as well, Mr. Cress," she said, matching his
politeness with a nod.

She made the mistake of looking up to find his
grayish-blue eyes resting on her.

Their gazes locked.

She felt drawn to him and felt the now-familiar hum
that gave voice to their chemistry. She knew he felt it,
as well. Several times over the last few weeks, she had
looked up to find his gaze *just* shifting away from her.

Setting a trap, whether he meant to do so or not.
Fueling her longing.

Monica forced herself to look away.

Moments later, the sound of his Italian leather shoes
tapping against the hardwood floors as he walked away
was a relief to her senses. Rubbing her hands against
the front of her black uniform pants, she walked over
to the glass wall and looked down at the backyard.
She squinted and leaned in to better see Lucas walk-

ing away from Jillian, who stood by the garden of fresh herbs in her white chef's coat.

Was the youngest Cress brother Jillian's secret lover, who wrote the note?

The taste of you still lingers on my tongue.

She looked on as Jillian watched Lucas's retreat, shook her head and bent her frame to pick herbs to place in the basket at her feet. Bitten by curiosity she knew she should resist, Monica rushed across the wide den to the stairwell, where her feet ate up the steps like she was trying to win a race. Reaching the first floor, she paused upon seeing Gabe and Lucas reaching the front door and didn't move until they exited.

Monica had just reached the dining room at the rear of the first floor when Jillian entered with her basket on her arm. Monica eyed the tall and slender bronzed beauty with her auburn curly hair pulled up into a top-knot. The chef's tortoiseshell spectacles didn't hide the long and thick lashes framing her round brown eyes. Her cheekbones were high and her chin narrow, giving her face a heart shape that brought emphasis to her full pouty mouth, which was painted crimson.

Jillian was pretty. And smart. And talented.

Just which of the Cress men had found it hard to ignore her appeal?

"Good morning, Chef Jillian," Monica said with a warm smile. "Busy?"

Jillian chuckled. "Good morning. And yes. Always," she said. "Lucas just threw a last-minute, picnic-lunch request at me for him and a date."

Well, that answers that.

"But what can I do for you?" the chef asked as she moved around the long dining room table for ten, topped with charcoal leather and surrounded by steel blue suede armless chairs.

"N-nothing," Monica stumbled. "Just taking a little break and thought I'd check on you."

Jillian gave her a polite smile. "I'll be honest, Monica, I'm too swamped for much girl talk today," she said with another a look of regret before swiftly walking into the kitchen to set the basket on the island.

"No problem. Another day," Monica said, already turning toward the elevator to ride back up to the fourth floor.

Lucas wouldn't make a lunch date and then ask his secret lover to prepare the food? Would he?

"Hmm," she said aloud.

Monica thought of the youngest Cress brother's steady merry-go-round of beauties since he'd lost fifty pounds and gone from chubby to chiseled in the last year. In fact, she remembered seeing him sneak one woman out of the house early one morning and catching him sneaking another in later that night.

He had only wiggled his eyes in mirth at her wide-eyed shocked expression as he hurried his "date" into his suite.

With *him* anything was possible.

Back in Gabe's suite, she was able to finish making his bed with fresh linens and tidy the sitting area and walk-in closet only by forcing herself to focus, pinching her wrists anytime her mind became occupied by naughty thoughts of the man with the name of an angel.

Monica rolled her cleaning caddie behind her to take the elevator to the third level, entirely devoted to Phillip Sr. and Nicolette. To her, it was the most beautifully luxurious space of the entire town house. As always, she paused in the doorway and took in the pure elegance of the massive bedroom, sitting room and office space, all flowing seamlessly from one room to the next, with elaborately carved wooden doors that blocked the views of the en suite bathroom and walk-in closets. The decor, flowers and plants, elaborate accessories, and the light streaming through the glass wall made for a stunning look.

It was like the glamorous set of a 1940s movie.

For a moment she pictured herself dressed in a satin gown with perfectly coiffed hair, large diamond baubles and painted with elaborate makeup, smoking from a long and slender cigarette holder as she blew perfect rings in succession.

The idea made her chuckle.

Allowing herself a quick stretch, Monica pulled on a fresh set of gloves and set about putting the room back to showcase status. She smoothed out any wrinkles in the gray coverlet before she folded it down to the edge of the king-size bed. She turned and noticed the edge of a folder sticking out from the mirror-trimmed antique nightstand. Normally she didn't venture inside private spaces, but she didn't want it to appear that she ignored her duties. She pulled the drawer out just enough to ease the folder back inside but found resistance when she tried to close it. She tried twice more with a frown. It felt off track.

Monica pulled the drawer out again to get it back on track. An inadvertent glance down revealed a typed sheet atop the file. She gasped as it registered just what she was seeing, and she rushed to ease the drawer closed. But then she thought one of the Cress parents would know she'd seen the file, and that could lead to her dismissal, so she quickly took the drawer back off track and tried her best to place the file peeking out just the way she'd found it.

She'd rather be admonished for overlooking the drawer than fired and kicked out on the street for seeing that one of the Cress parents—maybe both— currently had their family under surveillance by a private detective.

They were wealthy and powerful but still human, and there was no such thing as a perfect human being. Nor perfect parents. Or family.

Not that she had much experience with one of her own.

But she knew she would rather tackle her loneliness than be in a family that was slowly shifting as the sons all vied for their father's position as Cress, INC.'s CEO. In the six months since Phillip Sr. had first alluded to stepping down, the closeness she'd witnessed between the five brothers was beginning to fade. That troubled her, but she was a hired employee and said nothing about the more frequent arguments, the sly observa- tions of another brother's missteps or failures whenever they were in their father's presence, or the decline in family events over the last few months.

Even the night of the celebration, Gabe had left the rest of the family behind to party alone.

It is none of my concern. It's my job to clean up their physical messes. Not the emotional ones. I just hate they don't know how blessed they are to have each other. I wish I had—

She pushed away that long-held regret, refusing to give any more energy to her grief over her parents not wanting her for their own.

Quickly, Monica finished her duties and was glad to leave. She had just peeled back a veil to the Cress family that she could not unsee. With that, she no longer viewed them as a loving, close-knit family.

"Gabe, Gabe, Gabe."

The memory of that night and his name tumbling from Monica's lips with a passion she couldn't hide had him in a trance. So much so that he didn't even see the Manhattan skyline outside the floor-to-ceiling windows of his office in the Cress, INC. headquarters in Midtown. Instead, in the reflection, he visualized a scene of him making love to Monica playing out before him.

And that had been nearly a constant during the last three weeks.

Monica had surprised him that night and left him impressed with her ardor. The passion.

Still, no matter how delicious their tryst, it had been a one-time treat. He wasn't interested in anything more with the shy beauty and her hidden hunger. Nothing could ever be between them but hot sex, and he was willing to honor her request for a one-night stand.

"Just this once. Then I better make it damn good."

"Please."

Gabe had learned long ago the leap from good sex to love was easier for some women than most men. And his gut told him Monica Darby was that type. He had no love to give, and he would never want to lead her on when he knew he was just as adamant about his success as he was in avoiding a serious relationship. His romantic history had proven he was unable to balance the expectations of both love and his career without anyone suffering.

Most important, he was fully aware his mother would fire Monica if she discovered their tryst. Common sense said Monica needed her job, and he'd much rather have the trustworthy and efficient woman as their reliable housekeeper than his temporary bedmate. Anything else was selfish on his part.

I can't believe I almost messed it all up, he thought.

Not that it hadn't been one hell of a night.

They'd both agreed that they should put the night behind them and move on as if it had never happened.

It's for the best.

Still, he was quite tired of waking up from erotic dreams of her and taking cold showers to ease his desire.

Bzzzzzz.

Gabe cleared his throat and turned in his chair to face his ebony-wood desk. He pressed the intercom button. "Yes," he said briskly, flexing his agile fingers before turning to type his password to access his laptop.

"Your brother Phillip Jr. is here," his assistant said, her voice echoing through the speakerphone of the system.

"Gabe, Gabe, Gabe."

"Send him in," he said, ignoring the sultry memory that seemed akin to the enchanting whispers of one of Homer's Sirens. Although he didn't want to admit it, he was thankful to his brother for intruding on thoughts of Monica he knew he had no right having.

Phillip Jr. opened the door and strolled in, closing it behind him. "I heard you and Lucas went to look at a new factory for the cookware line," he said, his deep voice booming.

It matched his tall muscular frame. He lived up to the comparison to former wrestler turned actor Dwayne "The Rock" Johnson. To tease him, the brothers would all mimic The Rock's signature wrestling line: *Can you smell what The Rock is cooking?* Tongue wiggle and all.

"Yes. He wanted my advice," he said, going to the website of the James Beard Award to scroll down to announced nominees in the categories for restaurants and chefs before briefly glancing over at his brother.

"After he asked me for it first and then left me hanging? Or were you two plotting against me?" Phillip Jr. asked, coming to stand behind one of the chairs lined in front of the desk and gripping the back of one of them so tightly Gabe feared his fingers would burst through the leather.

Gabe leaned back in his chair and eyed his brother. "In what way, Philly?" he asked, purposely reverting to his brother's childhood nickname.

It served his purpose to disarm him.

Phillip Jr.'s stance softened. "Maybe the two of you think you stand a better chance at Dad's favor as a team," he said.

Gabe shook his head. "I don't like to share anything. You know that," he said.

"And I don't like being the eldest—his damn *namesake*—and being overlooked," Phillip volleyed back, once again voicing his opinion that he should automatically inherit the throne.

Gabe remained quiet. He wanted to be named CEO, but he refused to fight with his brothers to obtain the title. It was a horrible use of time, intelligence and energy.

Phillip released a derisive chuckle filled with his frustration before turning to take long strides to the closed door to jerk it open. He paused in the frame. "Good luck on the nominations *next* year," he said before taking his leave.

That last shot did cause Gabe to shift in his seat. None of the Cress restaurants had received a nod.

In the past, the family used to gather together for the announcement of the nominees to celebrate or commiserate together. Now he didn't know if his brother truly wished him well the next time or if he'd let his blind ambition make a loss a reason to gloat to their father as proof of Gabe's inability to lead the empire.

Sad times.

Gabe wiped his mouth with his hand as he closed his eyes and released a long breath. He wanted to win the coveted seat, as well, but to what end? This wasn't a nighttime soap opera where hurt and misdoings could be erased or lessened with the stroke of a writer's pen.

What was happening to the *family* in their family empire?

Bzzzzzz.

He glanced at his watch and his body tensed, even as he reached over to hit the intercom button once more. "Yes?"

"Lunch is served, Mr. Cress."

Gabe drummed his fingers atop his desk. "Thank you," he replied, wishing he had anywhere else to be.

Absolutely *anywhere*.

He eyed his stocked bar and contemplated a double pour of brandy but decided against it. He needed to be sharp. The verbal daggers were about to fly.

Cress, INC.'s corporate offices occupied the entire fortieth floor of the towering building, and there was a test kitchen nestled among the dozen offices and conference rooms. It had become tradition when his mother wasn't busy at her acclaimed cooking school for her to fix lunch for the family and support staff. Normally he looked forward to his mother's cuisine, but of late, the family gatherings could be a bit dicey and swing anywhere between loving and challenging.

The scent of tomatoes and seafood was heavy in the air. Admittedly his stomach rumbled, but he didn't quicken his pace to the family's private dining area that was separate from the one for the employees. Barbara, one of the company's office staff, gave him an appreciative eye as they came toward each other in the hall leading to the test kitchen.

"That's a beautiful tie, Mr. Cress," she said with a sly smile as she came to a stop in front of him, effectively blocking his path.

Barbara had made it clear over the years that she was open to more than a work relationship, but Gabe had always maintained a professional distance. Today would be no different. "Thank you," he said with a polite nod that he knew was stiff. "Enjoy your lunch."

"Care to join me?" she asked.

Gabe opened his mouth.

"Sorry, Babs, but my big brother has a lunch date with me."

Gabe glanced back at his brother Cole, a near look-alike for the actor Michael Ealy, strolling up to them dressed in jeans, boots and a long-sleeved black T-shirt. Ever the rebel of the family, Cole ignored their parents' request for their sons to wear office attire. Just as his insistence on operating his food truck during the weekends was a thorn in their father's side.

"Another time, then," the petite and pretty woman said with another lingering look up at him before walking away.

As she passed Cole, he stopped to turn his head to watch her.

"Careful, little brother," Gabe warned and then silenced any further admonishments as he remembered his own recent tryst with an employee.

"Gabe. Gabe. Gabe."

Cole finally turned to reach his side and they continued up the hall together.

"Maybe she'll turn her attention to you," Gabe said.

"She can play with the fire if she wants," Cole said. "*I'm* not the good one who wouldn't dare break a rule."

The Good One.

His brothers had often teased him for being a Goody Two-shoes.

"Just once. Then I better make it damn good."

Funny. He'd been very good at breaking the rules that night.

Gabe bit back a smile at the memory.

"Hundred dollars, it's *fideuà*," Cole said as they reached the double wooden doors to the family's private dining room.

Gabe paused. "Paella," he said.

Cole nodded. "Bet."

They entered the brightly lit room of modern design to find everyone else already assembled around the large round set table.

"Damn," Cole swore at the sight of the big and wide frying pan of paella in the center of the table on top of a large trivet.

Gabe took the folded hundred-dollar bill from between his brother's index and middle fingers to slide into his pocket before claiming a seat in between Phillip Jr. and Lucas. The aromatic dish was filled with lobster, mussels, clams and shrimp. Steam still rose from it.

"The paella smells good, Ma," Sean said, removing

the linen napkin atop his gold-rimmed plate and opening it across his lap.

"Ton père a préparé le déjeuner pour nous aujourd'hui," Nicolette told them, knowing her husband and sons spoke both French and Spanish fluently.

Their father had cooked.

The Cress brothers all paused and shared brief looks surreptitiously before watching their father's tall and solid frame move around the table as he filled everyone's goblet with a vintage white wine.

Gabe was sure their thoughts were in alignment with his own. There was no coincidence between their father cooking lunch at work—something he had never done—and the James Beard Award nominations being announced and the family coming up nil in the journalism and restaurant-and-chef categories. In their separate careers as chefs, nearly all of them had been nominated or won as Outstanding Restaurateur or Best Chef. But as a collective under the umbrella of Cress, INC. the accolade had yet to be received.

Phillip Leonard Cress Sr. was not pleased by that fact.

And him cooking such a nuanced meal that took skill, knowledge and use of many techniques to create the Spanish dish correctly—perfectly—was an unspoken reminder that he expected nothing less from his sons than excellence. Earning prestigious awards for Cress, INC. would serve as a testament to the quality of the business.

Phillip Sr. served each of his family members before raising his wine goblet into the air. *"À la nourriture. À la vie. À l'amour,"* he said before claiming his seat next to his wife.

Everyone tasted the paella.

Gabe fought not to close his eyes in pleasure at the exquisite seasoning, the tenderness of the seafood mix and the perfect, crunchy crust at the bottom of the rice dish. It was divine.

Just as Phillip Sr. knew it to be.

Message received.

Four

Two weeks later

Monica trembled so hard that the letter she held clutched in both her hands rattled as if unsettled by wind. But she was secure from the spring breezes inside the posh Manhattan law offices. It was her nerves that caused the tremble. The shock of it all.

"Miss Darby?"

She heard the attorney, but his voice sounded distant instead of that of a man across the desk from her. She released small breaths as she looked down at the skirt of her print dress, remembering how much she'd fretted if it was the right thing to wear to an appointment with a high-powered lawyer.

Especially when I didn't know what it was about at the time. I hope it's okay.

Monica knew her random thoughts were a diversion from the truth she'd just been told.

"Do you understand what I've explained?" he asked. "You've been left an inheritance by Brock Maynard—"

"The actor?" she asked, although he'd already given her his name. She shifted her eyes to the bald portly man with thick, framed spectacles. "In all the movies?"

"Yes," he nodded. "Your father."

Monica's lip curled as she shook her head. "Not my father. He was a sperm donor," she said snidely, feeling overcome with all the years of sadness and loneliness she had felt. For so long she had wondered who her parents were and why they hadn't been able—or wanted to—raise her. And she'd thought of everything. Even their deaths.

Discovering that her father was a wealthy and famous actor was worse.

Had been an actor. Now he's dead.

She looked around at the high ceilings, upscale decor and the New York skyline so clearly seen out the windows. This was the world of the Cress family and those of that ilk. Wealthy and affluent. Smart and talented. She could easily see Gabe sitting behind the desk with all the confidence and bravado needed to control the room.

She felt out of place. Like an intruder into *his* world.

Gabe.

Why am I thinking about him right now? Why am I always thinking of him?

She bit her bottom lip at the memory of their encounter beneath the twinkling fairy lights entwined among the flowers of the pergola.

Because I can't forget that night.

"Miss Darby."

You're beautiful.

"Miss Darby?"

Monica cut her eyes back at the attorney. "Yes?" she answered with a simplicity that made her wonder if she had lost her mind.

Yesterday afternoon FedEx had delivered a letter requesting her presence at the law offices of Curro Villar and Hunt. She'd looked them up, saw that they were reputable—and not attorneys hired as creditors— and called to make her appointment with Marco Villar as requested.

That's his name. Villar. Marco Villar.

And now, nearly five minutes later—maybe more than that—after being escorted into his posh offices in her inexpensive dress from a discount store, by a towering beauty who could be a model, Monica was still held fixated by a blend of confusion, shock and, yes, hurt.

"There is just one provision to receive the money," Mr. Villar said.

Something in his dark eyes behind the glasses let her know his next words would hurt. She stiffened her back and notched her chin.

"You must sign a nondisclosure agreement—"

Monica released a bitter laugh as she jumped to her feet. "The final insult," she said, her voice soft. "Not wanting to claim me even in death."

She turned and quickly walked across the wide breadth of his office.

"Monica!"

She turned, surprised by the feminine voice that called her name. A petite woman in an emerald green pantsuit was standing in the doorway of a room just off Marco Villar's office. She clutched her purse so tightly that her brown skin thinned over her knuckles.

"Now what?" Monica asked.

Mr. Villar rose to his feet, but the woman held up her hand and shook her head as she kept her attention on Monica. "We didn't mean to trick you or anything, Monica," she said loudly, her voice raspy as if she lived off cigarettes. "I am Brock's sister, Phoebe. Your aunt, if you will."

Monica stepped back with widening eyes and released a small gasp of surprise as the woman neared her. "We look alike," she said, her eyes missing no details of the woman, who was in her sixties or seventies.

Phoebe smiled. "Technically, you look like me," she said.

A famous father? A look-alike aunt? An inheritance?

"Ladies, why don't you have a seat," Marco said, coming from behind his desk to wave them both over to his sitting area. "Help yourself to a drink from the bar and I'll give you a moment."

With that he left them alone.

Phoebe sat down and crossed her ankles as she patted the seat on the leather sofa beside her.

"What do you want with me?" Monica asked as she remained standing.

"I hate what my brother did to you, and had I known about you, I would have raised you myself," she said, her eyes filling with tears as she pressed a wrinkled brown hand to her chest. "He told me on his deathbed, and it took every bit of willpower I have in this small body not to reveal to my dying brother that his treatment of you angered and disappointed me. It forever changed my view of the man I thought him to be. I *swear* to you. I didn't know."

Her anguish was clear, and Monica did not have the heart to ignore that. She took the seat beside her and let the woman reach for her hands to clasp them tightly between her own.

"When Marco told me they located you, I begged him to let me hide here so that I could see you. I didn't know if you'd even want to meet me, once I learned of all the challenges you had to overcome in your life," Phoebe said. "But I couldn't let you leave and walk away from what he owes you, Monica. It is the least he could do, to give you an easier life than you've had these last thirty years."

"But even in death, he won't claim me," she said, her voice hollow. Her heart hurting.

"That money is yours to do with as you see fit," Phoebe said, her voice fiery and passionate. "If you sign those papers, collect that money and say to hell with all of us, I wouldn't blame you one bit."

"So *you* want me to sign the NDA, too?" she asked, easing her hands out of the woman's grasp.

Phoebe swiped away the tears with her hands. "I didn't know about it until Marco said it, but to get your money? Yes!" she exclaimed. "You may have to sign an NDA to get your money, but I don't. I can speak your truth even if you can't. Your presence will not be denied anymore. I promise you that! Hell, I would do it even if I lost the stipend he left me to maintain the beach house he purchased for me years ago in Santa Monica."

"In California?" she asked, still trying to process the entire thing.

"And guess what?" Phoebe said, reaching again for her hands. "He named you after one of his favorite places in the world."

"He named me?" Monica asked.

"A small gesture to appease his guilt, I guess."

Was I so hungry for love that such a small gesture mattered that much to me?

"And my mother?" Monica asked.

"I know the story of your birth but not her name. That, he wouldn't reveal," Phoebe said with obvious regret. "But I'm sure there must be a way to find her. Perhaps Marco and his team could help with it."

Was I ready to find my mother? I wasn't sure. It could be just more sadness and disappointment.

"We'll see. I need some time to process all of this," Monica said.

Her aunt nodded in understanding. "I hope you'll give me a chance to get to know you, Monica."

"Perhaps…in time. I can't make any promises," she said.

"I will leave my contact info with Marco and when— or if—you're ready, you can get it from him," Phoebe offered. "Just know there is no deadline on when you reach out to me. Be it a day or a year or a dozen—if I'm still alive, God willing—I will accept you with open arms."

Monica remained silent.

Phoebe rose to her feet to summon the attorney back to his office. "She's ready," she said.

Am I?

As Monica rose and moved across the spacious divide to the attorney's desk with her newfound aunt at her side, she longed for a moment of solitude to let it all sink in. She listened to his explanation of the NDA even as she continued to stare over his shoulder out the window.

She had so many more questions.

Do I have siblings?

Was he married?

What is this story of my birth?

When is the funeral? Am I invited to attend?

Who is my mother?

But she was not ready to absorb one more piece of info.

Not today. Except...

"Exactly how much is the inheritance?" she asked after Marco finished calling one of the clerks at the firm who was a notary public.

Marco looked to Phoebe briefly as he crossed his hands over the papers on his neat desk. "Fifty million dollars."

"Huh?" she asked, blinking so swiftly that it appeared to be rapid gunfire before her eyes. "Fifteen million?"

Both Marco and Phoebe chuckled.

"No. *Fifty* million, not fifteen," he said with emphasis.

She felt light-headed and willed herself not to faint to the floor and send the billowy skirt of her thin dress up over her head.

Gabe looked up at the top of the illuminated Eiffel Tower in the distance as he leaned in the doorway of CRESS V in the Champs-Élysées area of Paris. He was a Manhattanite who enjoyed the fast pace and urban flair of the city for sure, but the City of Lights, or *la Ville Lumière*, was a close second. It was where his mother had been born, where his parents had met and home to his favorite style of cuisine. He was staying at his parents' country estate in the village of Saint-Germain-en-Laye for the week while he scouted possible locations for a new Cress restaurant.

The flute of champagne he nursed was unrivaled in its quality and well worth its hefty cost. That evening though, the restaurant was closed for a private celebration, and because of the event the liquor was apropos.

Finishing his drink with a small grunt of pleasure, he turned and opened the glass door to step back inside the restaurant. The entire staff was gathered in celebration of the release of the tenth cookbook by its head chef and Gabe's best friend, Lorenzo León Cortez. He was well loved and respected by his staff and his peers.

"You look exhausted, friend," Lorenzo said, giving

him a quick look over the rim of the bottle of beer he nursed as Gabe neared him. "Who is she?"

Monica.

Gabe shook his head, refraining from revealing to even his best friend that he'd slept with the family's housekeeper. "I'm on a little break from sex," he admitted.

Lorenzo scoffed. "Medical issues?" he joked.

He gave his friend a look that was reproachful before shaking his head. "A one-night stand has had me in a loop for the past month," he admitted.

"Ah. The one-night stand that's really not just one night," Lorenzo said, looking wistful. "I've had a few of those in my lifetime."

"Yes, but it was just one night," Gabe confessed.

Lorenzo winced and then released a short whistle. "Then at the very least have one more night, bro," he said.

One more wild night with Monica?

Maybe, just maybe, that would quench his desire for her. Or make him want her even more.

No. Monica Darby was off-limits. They couldn't risk it again. It was just the thing to get her fired.

And me hooked.

"Sometimes you make me very envious, Zo," Gabe said, purposely changing the subject.

"Why? Because I have three inches of height on you?" Lorenzo asked, shifting his bone-straight, waist-length hair back behind his broad shoulders.

Gabe chuckled. "I have the extra inches where it

counts," he said before pouring himself half a glass of the golden champagne.

"*Way* more info than I needed," Lorenzo drawled. "But what's on your mind? Or should I guess?"

"We talk. It wouldn't be hard to guess. Not for you," he said, turning to face the large window into the kitchen, usually bustling with activity.

"You miss cooking," Lorenzo said with a brief glance over his shoulder.

Gabe nodded. "Sometimes more than other times," he admitted. "Don't get me wrong. I am so proud of the legacy we are building for Cress generations to come. These last three years at Cress, INC. has been eye-opening and challenging, *but…*"

"There is nothing like the adrenaline rush of heading a kitchen. Right, Chef?"

Gabe glanced over at his friend and then fixed his gaze back on the kitchen. "Correct, Chef," he returned.

A sudden surge in laughter caused both men to look over at the waitstaff having an impromptu dance contest.

"And what of the race for CEO, then?" Lorenzo asked him, leaving the staff to their fun.

"I want that, too," he stressed.

"In this not-so-perfect world, you can't always have everything you want, Gabe."

True.

Lorenzo nudged Gabe's arm and then slightly jerked his head in the direction of the double doors leading into the kitchen. As soon as they stepped inside the massive space, he grabbed two aprons from the stacks of clean ones on polished wooden shelves by the door. He tossed one to his friend with ease.

Gabe caught it with one hand and a curious look.

"If you could make any dish in the world right now what would it be?" Lorenzo asked as he tied the strings around his waist.

Gabe did the same. "You have an entire buffet of food out there."

"We are open six nights a week, and this is the first night I had time to celebrate my new cookbook, and tonight I would like Gabriel Cress, esteemed chef, my former head chef, two-time–James Beard Award winner and my best friend since culinary school, to cook a meal for me," Lorenzo said, waving his hand toward the huge walk-in cooler in the corner. "What can I get you, Chef?"

"And you'll be my sous-chef? Interesting," Gabe said as he moved to one of the sinks to wash his hands.

"Yes, but it will be like your mystery woman…one night only," Lorenzo said with a laugh as he gathered his hair at his nape with a black elastic band and then washed his hands, as well.

"Do you remember the dish that made Chef Roderick give me dish duties for a week?" Gabe asked.

"Do I!" Lorenzo said, shaking his head as he began retrieving pots.

For the next thirty minutes, Gabe allowed himself to think of nothing but his love of food, from prep to completion. Even as the music and the laughter of the staff filtered in to them, he was in a zone. It was an adrenaline rush, and his friend was the perfect sous-chef following every command and at times having the next item prepared for him even before he requested it. To Gabe it was the perfect symphony.

Soon the scent of his goat-cheese-and-roasted-butternut-squash bisque rose strong in the air. He used his hand to waft the aroma closer to his face and took a deep inhale. His cell phone vibrated in his back pocket, but he ignored it. With a plastic spoon he tasted the bisque before adding a large pinch from the bowl of pink Himalayan salt.

Moving with a rhythm that was fluid and precise, he cut the kernels from the cobs of corn Lorenzo grilled and added them, as well.

"Ravioli, Chef," Lorenzo said, sliding over the tray of handmade, dried ravioli he'd stuffed with ricotta, lump crab meat, parmesan and wild mushrooms.

Gabe gave him a brisk nod even as he focused on spooning the pasta into the boiling water. Ten minutes later, he ladled the bisque into a large family-style ceramic bowl before adding the ravioli using a long-handled skimmer. He shredded fresh parmesan and quickly chopped scallions to scatter across the top.

With a nod of satisfaction, he set the bowl before Lorenzo, who at some point had poured himself a large glass of red wine. "Enjoy," Gabe said, stepping back and wiping his sweaty brow with the hand towel he had tucked inside the waist of his apron.

It was only then that he noticed the staff had wandered into the kitchen to observe him as he was cooking. He smiled as he saw the looks of admiration on many of their young faces. He had been so lost in his art.

"Well?" Gabe asked Lorenzo.

Everyone turned to him to gauge his reaction.

His friend took care to scoop an entire ravioli covered with bisque before spooning the steamy food into his mouth. He closed his mouth and released a little grunt of pleasure as he chewed. "I see you learned the lesson Chef Roderick taught you very well," he said. *"Es la perfección, amigo mío."*

"Gracias." Gabe thanked him with a nod as applause exploded around him at his friend saying the dish was perfection.

They all quickly moved to indulge themselves in consuming the dish, and he took time to watch the pleasure wash over their faces at their initial bites. It felt like the first time he knew he had the skill and the talent to make delicious food.

He retrieved a goblet and slid it over to his friend to fill.

"Here's to one night only," Lorenzo said with a wink.

Gabe toasted to that, thinking of another one-night stand that was unforgettable.

One week later

Life was surreal.

Monica awakened in her housekeeper's quarters as always. She showered and dressed in her uniform, prepared to begin her daily chores. In her all-white bathroom, she took a moment to study her reflection.

For five years this had been her life. Here with the Cress family. On the perimeter but still one among many. It was the most stability she'd ever known. What with growing up in foster care and then traveling with James, she had never had a chance to plant roots. It felt silly to worry about yet another new start when she had been blessed with so much money to do it with, but she did.

Same surroundings. Same tasks.

Different Monica.

She'd given her two weeks' notice to Mrs. Cress and was excited about the money, which was to clear her bank account the next day, but she was also nervous about leaving her home-that-wasn't-really-home next week, packing her personal items and forging ahead.

Alone again.

She saw the sadness and fear fill her eyes and turned away from it.

Was it silly that I'd rather have had my father back than his money now?

She made her way upstairs to the first level, and like any other day, the house was still and quiet. She took a moment to pause in the kitchen and slowly turn to take in everything in the early morning. Pockets of light from sconces and under-cabinet lighting gave it such a lovely glow. Even as she looked across the kitchen and adjoining dining room with its glass wall, the water-fall at the end of the garden was backlit and made the backyard appear magical as the sun began to rise in the metropolitan sky.

It was a beautiful home in an affluent neighborhood and she would miss it when she left.

What will Gabe think?

He'd been in Paris all week, and she didn't know if he knew her days at the Cress town house were nearing an end.

Pushing aside thoughts of him, Monica made herself a cup of coffee and had fresh fruit before moving throughout the entire first level ensuring no messes had been made by the family after she retired to her quarters last night. She chuckled, remembering during her first few weeks awakening to the aftermath of a late-night, spontaneous dinner party to top all dinner parties. Chaos had reigned and the empty plates and wine bottles had been abundant.

Thankfully all was well except for a random glass here or there, overturned pillows and a few filled wastepaper baskets that she emptied into a garbage bag. Lightly humming a tune, she carried that bag and those from the cans in the kitchen to the interior entrance and through the marbled vestibule to the outer door.

She paused halfway down the stairs and looked up the street at the rows of ornate townhomes. Next week, everything would change and she had some decisions to make. Home or condo. New York or New Jersey. Travel or…or…

Or what?

The sudden flash of cameras and raised voices caused her to turn her head. She froze and leaned back from the crowd advancing to surround the porch.

"There she is!"

"That's her!"

Monica's eyes widened in shock at the people pointing cameras up at her from the street. "What?" she asked, feeling her heart pound.

"Are you Monica Darby?" one of them yelled to her.

She climbed back up a step.

"How do you feel about the death of your father that you never knew?"

"Do you hate Brock Maynard?"

The bags dropped from her trembling hands.

"Why weren't you invited to the funeral?"

Their barrage of questions was rapid and overlapping. The flash of cameras and the steady beam of lights from the video cameras were shocking intrusions into her life.

"Were you mentioned in the will?"

"If you're not in the will, do you have plans to sue?"

"Move! Excuse me. Out of the way!" a male voice roared. Gabe pushed through the throng of paparazzi on the street with ease, holding his suitcase with one hand. She then noticed the family's SUV pulling off down the street.

He opened the wrought-iron gate to race up the stairs to her. She felt sweet relief when he slid his arm around her waist and turned her to guide her back up the stairs.

"How does it feel to go from being a maid to the daughter of an A-lister?"

Gabe ushered her into the vestibule, closed the door and set down his luggage.

"What is all that about?" Gabe asked as they entered the house. "What are they saying about your father? What's going on?"

Remembering her NDA, Monica pressed her lips closed and shrugged as she shook her head. Lines of annoyance filled his handsome face as he moved back to the door to look out the tinted glass panes at the photographers still there. She allowed herself a moment to take him in. To enjoy being near him for what was the last time. He looked so handsome in his denims and a crisp blue shirt that made his eyes all the more brilliant in his tanned shortbread complexion.

"I resigned from my position here last week and gave two weeks' notice," she began.

He turned his head to eye her. Confusion filled his face even as she gave him a brisk nod.

"But I think I should leave today," she said, enjoying the subtle hint of his warm and spicy cologne. Fireworks seemed to shoot off in her belly.

"Today?" he said, his voice deep.

She nodded. Her nondisclosure agreement kept her from explaining even more. It was the price of her inheritance.

"Is it because of what happened between us?"

"No."

"Do you have a better position?"

"No."

They shared a long look before he extended his hand. "I guess this is goodbye," he said.

Monica slipped her hand into his. "I guess so," she agreed, silently taking note how his large hand easily engulfed her own.

And felt so warm. Especially his thumb resting against her sensitive inner wrist.

She broke the hold, choosing to focus on calling the police to get rid of the crowd outside. The Upper East Side address would speed up their arrival.

"Monica. Wait."

"Yes, Mr. Cress?" she asked, turning to face him.

He bent down in front of his monogrammed Vuitton case to remove an envelope from the side pocket. "The Cress Family Foundation's charity ball is next week. I'd like for you and a guest to attend. *Please*," he stressed.

"I don't think that would be appropriate—" she began but then remembered that in less than twenty-four hours she would be worth just as much as he was and she would no longer be his maid.

He eyed her.

"I'll consider it," she conceded, taking the thick and creamy envelope from him. "Thank you."

With one last smile Monica turned from him to finish out her last day and make plans for her tomorrow.

Five

One week later

The Cress family is as surprised as the world at the news that our beloved Monica is the daughter of Brock Maynard. Although we were saddened to lose her as an invaluable and dedicated employee no longer living in our home, we do ask that the privacy of the entire Cress family be respected at this time since we have no further information to add to this conversation. In closing, we wish Monica the very best.

Gabe didn't bother to read the rest of the online newspaper story about Monica after finishing the family's official statement, released through the publicity team at Cress, INC. The hope was to thin out the paparazzi still driving through the neighborhood at slow speeds in hopes of catching a photo of Monica, who had already moved out of the home.

"Now hopefully *that* is the end of *that*," Nicolette said with emphasis.

He shifted his gaze from a spot outside in the garden over to his mother, sitting at one end of the dining room table. She slapped the folded newspaper she held on to the leather top of the table, beside her plate of fresh fruit and a buttery croissant. He knew without asking that she was speaking of something to do with their ex-employee, Monica.

It was all she'd seemed to want to discuss over the week since the paparazzi had camped outside their house and the press had revealed that Monica was in fact the secret love child of a famous actor. The fact that she worked as a maid made the story even more salacious.

"Time heals all things," Phillip Sr. said from the other end of the table before taking a deep sip of his cup of coffee.

Will time make me stop dreaming of her?

"I read on the *Star Gazette* her mother was a maid for her father when she got pregnant, and they gave her up for adoption and she came full circle by becoming a maid," Phillip Jr. said just before Chef Jillian walked in carrying a fresh carafe of the fresh-squeezed citrus juice they all loved.

She paused midstep at his words and frowned a little before continuing into the room to set the container on the table among the serving dishes of steaming food she'd prepared for them.

Gabe squeezed the bridge of his nose between his fingers, wishing his brother had more tact and less tongue on the matter. "Websites like the *Star Gazette* are hardly the place to get news," he said with censure. "We know firsthand they deal more in fiction than facts."

All he could remember was the fright in Monica's eyes as she was assailed by the paparazzi that morning. As his car pulled up before the house, he'd taken in the people outside before realizing it was Monica frozen in front of them, her eyes filled with fear and confusion. The desire to protect her had flooded him, and the car had barely stopped before he'd climbed out and barreled through the crowd to rush her back inside the house. He'd had to fight the impulse to swing and connect on the faces of those in the crowd.

"True. It's to be entertained…not informed," Cole drawled, reaching for a croissant to tear and dip in the homemade honey butter on his plate.

"Whatever," Phil muttered.

"Want some, Uncle Cole," Collette said from where she sat on her knees in the seat beside him.

He winked and honored her request as if her plate wasn't already stacked with pancakes shaped like Mickey Mouse. She giggled and proceeded to lick the decadent honey butter from the croissant.

All of the Cress men chuckled, finding her, as always, adorable.

Nicolette playfully scowled, and her mother, Raquel, gave Cole a reproachful look as she took the croissant and cleaned butter from her child's sticky fingers.

"Right, the *Gazette* also claims she's hidden away, using psychics to try to reconnect with her deceased father," Lucas agreed, nibbling his fresh fruit as he steered the convo back to Monica.

Gabe remained silent, allowing them to continue speculating on their ex-employee, who the press could not locate to harass. He had thoughts and questions of his own. Like why she hadn't told him the truth that morning.

"I resigned from my position here last week and gave two weeks' notice. But I think I should leave today."

"Today?"

"Is it because of what happened between us?"

"No."

"Do you have a better position?"

"No."

Gabe didn't know why Monica did not reveal more about her departure, but it was clear it involved the discovery of her parentage. *Or...she felt it was none of my business.*

"I am curious about where she disappeared to," Raquel said with a one-shoulder shrug. "Maybe she knew all along and didn't want to be found and that's why she's MIA."

"Who would choose to be a maid when her father is a rich actor?" Cole protested. "Sorry, Raquel, but that's ridiculous."

"Hell, the whole damn circus about the mess is ridiculous," Nicolette said. "But hopefully our inclusion in the drama is at its end, especially with the charity event tonight."

Bzzzzzz.

Gabe wiped his hands with his napkin before pulling his phone from the front pocket of his shirt to check the incoming call. Felicity. He did not answer.

"Is it even necessary to say tonight is not the night for the ladies you would not bring home to meet me?" Nicolette asked, piercing each son with her steely blue eyes. "And especially not the type who would willingly sneak into someone's home to lie up all evening doing God knows what with one of my horny sons. Right, Lucas?"

Raquel rushed to cover Collette's ears as the brothers laughed.

Lucas gave his mother his most charming smile. "Of course," he agreed.

Bzzzzzz.

He looked down at the screen of his phone. Felicity again. He could block her, ignore her calls or answer. His curiosity was piqued by the back-to-back calls so he chose the latter. "Hello, Felicity," he said, rising to leave the table with his cup of coffee to step outside to the garden.

"Hello, stranger."

She was in full-flirt mode right out the gate. He could hear it in her husky tones. She wanted something and not just to catch up. "How can I help you?" he asked, hoping to push the conversation forward.

"So businesslike, Gabriel."

He took a deep sip of the brew. "I haven't heard from you in a while, so I know there's something you want from me."

"Maybe I was reminiscing on the good times and missing you," she said.

"Or…"

She laughed. It was soft. Meant to allure.

"Or?" Gabe asked again, his voice echoing inside the cup.

"Gabriel, did we end on bad terms?" Felicity asked.

"We didn't technically end at all. We both just stopped calling each other," he said, checking the time on his watch. "That's a clear sign we both moved on, but if there is something I'm able to do for you, just ask."

"A ticket to tonight's charity event would be nice."

Gabe looked up to the sky in exasperation. *And there it is.*

"I won't be able to do it, Felicity," he said.

He hadn't decided whether to bring a date or not, and the last thing he needed was an impetuous ex to ruin his evening out of spite.

"Besides, I gave away my last two tickets," he added truthfully.

"Ga-bri-el," she said in a singsong manner. "It's *your* family's event. Surely you can get another ticket."

"My brother Phillip runs the foundation and is running the show on the ball. He told us over a week ago it was sold out," Gabe said.

"I think a ticket would just make me *sooo* grateful. I might lose my mind and do *anything* to show my appreciation," she said with a little moan. "You remember how I show my thanks, don't you, Ga-bri-el?"

He did.

Gabe cleared his throat. "Felicity, I can't help, but it was good hearing from you," he said.

"Was it?" she asked, her tone cool.

"Of course."

"Remember it well, because I doubt it will happen again."

She ended the call.

He finished off his coffee and reentered the house.

"Where in the world is... Monica Darby?"

His eyes followed that of his entire family to the sizable television over the fireplace in the den that was on other side of the chef's kitchen. A morning entertainment-news show was on, and the mention of the ex-housekeeper's name had caught everyone's attention.

He eyed the video of Monica on the television before reclaiming his seat at the table. Her eyes were round and wide as she stood frozen on the steps of their town house.

"There's our house on television! When will this madness end? Merde!" Nicolette swore in French.

"The secret love child of Academy Award–winning actor of stage and film Brock Maynard has not been seen since this day, leaving the Upper East Side town house of the Cress family who are well-known for their culinary empire...and their good looks. Take a look at this family!"

The family's publicity shot filled the screen.

Nicolette groaned.

Phillip Sr. frowned.

Sean smiled broadly.

Phillip Jr. released a heavy breath.

Cole laughed.

Lucas winced.

Gabe tightened his jaw as the image changed to the flashes of the cameras playing over Monica's face. He wondered about her whereabouts. Was she okay? Was she happy? He hoped so because she deserved it. She had been nothing but trustworthy and reliable as the lone regular employee in their home. He wished her nothing but the best. He thought of the tickets to the ball he'd given her and admitted that he hoped she'd decided to attend.

"We may not be able to zone in on Monica Darby's whereabouts, but we have recently learned from a trusted source that Maynard did indeed leave his estate, estimated to be worth more than fifty million dollars, to his daughter. Now, that's how you say sorry..."

That info stunned the entire Cress family.

The last week had been absolutely chaotic.

Monica sat on the foot of the king-size bed of her guest room of the luxury hotel on Fifth Avenue as she used the remote to flip through the cable channels. She paused at the sight of the video of her looking frightened that had been overused the last week, online and on television. "Now what?" she muttered.

"The secret love child of Academy Award–winning actor of stage and film Brock Maynard has not been seen since this day, leaving the Upper East Side town house of the Cress family who are well-known for their

culinary empire...and their good looks. Take a look at this family!"

Monica's eyes went to Gabe's face in the photo. Nothing had changed in the week since she'd last seen him. The very sight of him still made her feel more alive than the moment before.

She looked over at the opened envelope on the dresser, holding the tickets to the charity event. An opportunity to see him once more. "Should I?" she mouthed.

"We may not be able to zone in on Monica Darby's whereabouts, but we have recently learned from a trusted source that Maynard did indeed leave his estate, estimated to be worth more than fifty million dollars—"

Click.

Monica tossed the remote behind her onto the bed after having cut off the television. "Trusted source?" she protested. "You mean Phoebe Maynard? Then just say that."

It was indeed her aunt that had planted the stories with the press because she refused to allow her brother to do in death what he'd done when he was alive—pretend he didn't have a daughter. And Monica appreciated the show of support from Phoebe, but it had sent the press into her life with the vengeance of bees whose nest had been knocked to the ground.

She was tired of being stung.

With a sigh she moved across the room to the dresser and picked up the invite and pressed it to her nose. With every passing day the scent of his cologne lessened and now it barely held a hint of the warm and spicy aroma. She shifted her eyes up to see herself in the mirror, dressed in the luxury hotel's plush white cotton robe, with her hair pulled up into a messy top-knot, face free of makeup and her eyes bright with the light thinking about Gabe brought to them.

For the last week she had stayed cooped up in the posh hotel room in Midtown Manhattan, where the wealthy played, intending to remain until she'd made some final decision on where to start the newest chapter in her life. Every well-appointed detail of the room with its high ceilings, stylish decor and city view of Central Park was now imprinted on her brain.

No work. No guests. Nothing to keep her occupied. Nothing but her thoughts. And room service.

"Why let boredom be the death of me?" she asked, tapping the envelope against her chin as she decided it was time to have a little fun.

The next few hours were a whirlwind in Manhattan. Behind oversize shades, she ventured out of her room, and thankfully she faded into the fast-walking crowd with ease. Armed with advice from the concierge, she ventured to a nearby boutique, where she enjoyed try-ing on designer gowns until she found the one that made every eye in the shop stay on her. Diamond ear-rings from Van Cleef. Shoes from Bergdorf Goodman. Hair, makeup and manicure by the spa at the hotel.

Aside from the cost of the hotel, it was the first of her inheritance she'd dared to spend. And what felt trepid at first got a little easier with each swipe of the card connected to one of several bank accounts she'd opened. It felt odd to spend such an amount when before it would have taken weeks to earn that much, but it had felt good—for once—to treat herself. Not even a sales clerk asking her to provide photo ID to prove it was indeed her card had shaken her. She'd shown her identification and then left the store to spend her money elsewhere.

And now I'm here.

Monica looked out the tinted window from her seat in the rear of the chauffeur-driven Tahoe, taking in the entrance to the marina. It was beautiful at night with the moon's light reflecting on the gentle waves of the Hudson River. The lights from the towering buildings in the distance gave the perfect New York backdrop. When the SUV pulled to a stop in the parking lot, she forced herself to wait for the driver to leave his seat and come around to open the door.

"Thank you," she said, accepting the offer of his hand to help her from the sizable vehicle.

"Have a good night, Ms. Darby."

Ms. Darby? That flustered her for a moment. Everything felt new and different. Even experiencing a show of respect.

With a nod, she took a deep inhale of the scent of the river. Attendees clad in elegant evening wear were already making their way down the wharf toward the sleek two-hundred-foot navy megayacht docked on the other side of the marina. She smiled at their excited chatter—a clear sign of everyone's anticipation of the festivities.

A warm breeze blew in from the river as Monica stopped to look up at the yacht. The party was already in full swing and the music echoed from inside the three-tier vessel.

She knew from overhearing the family discuss the preparations that more than five hundred people were scheduled to attend the event. There should be a live band, open bar, decadent hors d'oeuvres, a silent auction of more than fifty culinary experiences with acclaimed chefs, a charity poker tournament, and a grand finale with a popular celebrity performing a miniconcert.

Aboard the yacht, with her heart pounding from excitement and a bit of nervousness, she went straight to the bar for a glass of champagne. Over the rim she took in the mingling crowd and the entertainers among them. Contortionists, magicians and jugglers performed for the crowd amid colorful decor, lighting effects and towering floral arrangements.

A uniformed server presented her a tray. She selected a small plate and used tongs to choose a bacon and chèvre tart, lamb lollipop and a mini potpie she soon discovered was filled with lobster. She was looking about the colorfully lit room when she spotted Gabe standing by the bar, looking devastatingly beautiful in an all-black tuxedo that fit him so very well. She nearly choked on her bite of food when she finally noticed the tall and shapely brunette in a strapless cerise jumpsuit beside him. *His date?*

The woman in red laughed as she stroked the velvet lapel of his tuxedo and removed the flute from his hand to press her crimson lips to the crystal for a deep sip of the golden champagne. Monica turned away from the sight so quickly that she felt loose waves of her hair tickle her spine. She hated how easy it was to notice how different she was in comparison to the woman. Even with the costly transformation that had given her confidence, Monica felt that familiar pang of being not good enough. A remainder of her broken and unstable childhood.

Needing to be out of Gabe and his sultry date's line of vision, Monica stopped another server to place her unfinished food and drink on his tray before she took her exploration elsewhere.

"Monica?"

A warm hand lightly wrapped around her wrist. She knew before she turned that it was Gabe. The goose bumps and soft hairs on her body standing on end were truth tellers. Facing him, she confirmed their accuracy. "Hello, Mr. Cress," she said, her heart racing as he eyed her from perfectly coiffed hair to painted toes.

Her black lace gown was delicate and sweet with its scalloped sweetheart bodice and bow-embellished straps, while still being sexy with her appearing to be nude underneath. The sheer A-line skirt showed hints of her thighs, and the lace border skimmed her ankles above the strappy heels she wore. Her hair was down in soft loose curls that passed her bare shoulders. Smoky eyes and a soft nude lipstick completed her look.

What does he think? she wondered.

"You…you look amazing," he said, his warm appreciation filling his voice.

She laughed softly. "You seem surprised," she teased.

"No. Not surprised," he said, easing his hands into

the pockets of his slacks. "I've seen you even prettier than this."

That made her cheeks warm.

Monica tucked her hair behind her ears, revealing dangling diamond earrings. "I wasn't sure if the dress was too much or not enough," she confessed.

Gabe's eyes were intense. "It's perfect," he admitted.

Their eyes locked and held. Silence reigned, but there was a charge—a current—that fueled the air between them. She knew from the heat in her belly and in his eyes that he felt the same stir of desire as she did. "*Just once.* Remember?" she reminded him as her pulse sprinted.

"I thought you forgot that night," he said, his gaze searching hers.

She looked away from him, seeking relief from his unspoken temptation. "We were supposed to."

"I couldn't forget it even when I tried."

She shivered.

"Look at me, Monica."

With an audible swallow over a lump in her throat, she did. And at that moment, she remembered a dozen different things about that night, from the feel of his hands gripping her buttocks to the way she'd moaned from the back of her throat in pleasure at his deep strokes.

"Excuse us?"

They looked to find a couple behind them. They'd not realized they were blocking the stairs.

Gabe grabbed her hand and pulled her behind him. Several times people called out to him or attempted to step in his path, but he bypassed them all as he led her up the stairs of the next two levels to the sundeck. As soon as they came to a stop, he pulled her body close to his and weaved his fingers through her hair as she tilted her chin up and clutched at the lapels of his tuxedo blazer. He lowered his head to kiss her.

First, a soft press of their lips together. Then, lightly touching their tongues in that hot little moment before the kiss deepened with moans that were guttural. His head leaned that way and hers the other. Their bodies pressed closely together.

The seconds seemed infinite. Monica ended the kiss with reluctance, not sure of how much time had passed from the very first feel of his mouth. She felt tipsy. And as if in a dream.

Her Prince Charming looked too delicious in his tailored tux for her not to long to undress him and have him for another night of passion.

Is it midnight? Will the carriage change back to a pumpkin? Have I lost my shoe?

She smiled at the whimsy.

"Just once more?" he asked, his voice deep and thrilling.

Her eyes fell to his mouth before she swiped the gloss from his lips with her thumb.

He eased his hands down to her lower back to gently knead the spot just above the curve of her buttocks. "You don't work for the family anymore," he said.

"No, I do not," Monica agreed, before stepping back out of his embrace and walking over to the railing to look out at the waves highlighted by the glow from the moon. She enjoyed the feel of the breeze, but it was nothing akin to the heat of Gabe's body.

He walked over to close the gap between them. "I'm not built for a relationship," he admitted.

"And I wouldn't want one with you," she countered, tilting her chin up a notch as she turned to lean back against the railing as he came to a stop before her.

"With just me? Or with anyone?" he asked, his voice as deep as the river surrounding them.

"Anyone. Love is for fools."

He chuckled and gripped the railing on either side of her body as he leaned down to press kisses from her chin to her lips. She released a telling gasp of pleasure.

"This thing between us is going to happen again," he said near her ear before shifting his head to taste her mouth.

Anticipation nearly made her weak. "Just…once… more," she spoke against his mouth.

Gabe stepped back from her and extended his hand. "Then let's get the hell out of here," he said.

Monica bit her bottom lip and smiled as she slid her hand in his.

The sun rose over Manhattan with ease, casting the city with light streaked with crimson, pinks and orange. Monica eyed the beauty outside the window of her hotel room as Gabe pressed warm kisses from one shoulder to the other. It was how he awakened her after a night of the most electric sex of her life.

First round was in one of the private cabins aboard

ship. That had been fast and furious, leaving them both sweaty and breathless.

Not done with each other, they used one of the family's cars to reach her suite, where the next round had been slow and passionate. Against the door. The floor. The sofa. The windowsill. And finally, the bed. At times he took the lead. Sometimes she was in charge.

Pure pleasure.

And now, from the length of his hardness against her buttocks, he was ready for round three.

She lay on her back, causing the sheet to twist down to her waist leaving her breasts exposed. She reached to pull it back up, now feeling shy under the light of day.

He shook his head before lowering it to suck one tight brown nipple into his mouth.

"It's morning," she gasped, even as her back seemed to arch up off the bed of its own accord. "We said just once more."

With one last delicious lick, Gabe freed her breast and looked down at her again. "Yes, but this part of me doesn't agree," he said, tightening the loose white sheet against his curving erection.

"She's regretting the deal we made, too," she said, giggling when he raised the sheet to look down at the smooth, flat hairs covering her vee.

Thank God for the waxing at the spa.

"Then maybe we need to do this again?" he asked, briefly locking his eyes with hers before he lay on his back and pulled her body so that she was atop him.

"Now?" she asked as she straddled him.

"And in the future."

She looked down at him, Gabriel "Gabe" Cress, and thought of all the nights over the last five years that she had only dreamed of having him naked and hard beneath her. She wasn't looking for love, because it was synonymous for heartbreak. But maybe she could just enjoy carnal pleasures knowing one day, when the heat cooled, they would just walk away and say a fond farewell? She had no doubt it would be very easy for him.

"No strings," she stated, mostly to let him know she was quite clear on the rules.

"None," he agreed, sitting up to lightly nuzzle her neck.

"The only thing I expect from you is great sex when I call," she teased, surprised at her boldness and liking it.

"And what about me?" he asked, his voice and his eyes smoldering.

Who have I become?

She felt naughty and flirty. Desirable and sexy. Was it her sudden wealth or the way she *knew* she made him feel? The only word for it was *powerful*.

Monica turned on his lap and then slid her body to all fours between his open legs. The bed dipped under his weight as moved to kneel behind her. She gripped the sheets and pressed her face against the bed as he eased his hardness inside her until nearly all of him filled her completely. They both hissed at the connection. With a wince and soft bite of her lip as Gabe reached around her to press his hand to her throbbing bud, she moved back and forth on his inches with a rotation of her hips when she reached the base.

Such a sinful glide. Meant to build a slow explosion in them both.

Ten glides—maybe less—and she felt him tremble with his release. He swore with force as she felt him harden even more inside of her. Like steel. That plus the smooth circular motions of his fingers against her caused her to cry out into the mattress and pound the softness with her fist as she joined him in sweet, white-hot bliss.

Six

The rules had been made. No long conversations on the phone. No official dates. No overnight stays. And they both held up their end of the arrangement. But that didn't stop the many hours they spent apart from being filled with thoughts of the other.

Gabe was consumed with constant memories of her at random spots of the day. The feel of her body. Her kisses. Her sighs against his mouth. And never knowing whether she would moan or release rough cries when she climaxed.

He made it his duty to get her yelling to the ceiling until her voice was hoarse.

That thought made him chuckle.

"What's funny, Gabriel?"

He looked up from the quarterly reports to find the entire board of Cress, INC. gazing down the table to where he sat, left of his father at the head. "A random thought," he explained.

"Care to share?" Nicolette asked from the other end of the oval-shaped conference table.

"Definitely not," he asserted.

The meeting carried on and Gabe was pleased. His family was blissfully unaware that their former housekeeper was his lover. His beautiful, smart, passionate and adventurous lover. Who he was ready to see. Smell. Touch. Taste.

"If there are no other new matters," Phillip Sr. began.

"Actually, is there an estimated date for when you will officially step down as chief executive officer and name a successor?" one of the board members asked.

Gabe looked on as his parents shared a glance across the length of the table. He also noted his eldest brother, Phillip Jr., seemed particularly pleased by the question. He twisted his favorite writing pen in his hand as he turned to his father for the answer to a question he was sure all of the Cress sons wanted to know. He certainly did.

"No, there is no estimated date, because I am not yet ready to step down," Phillip Sr. said.

Gabe frowned and fought the urge to shake his head as his grip on his pen tightened.

"Nor do I feel any of my sons are ready to step into my role," he added as he sat up straighter in his chair and folded his hands atop the table.

The frown deepened and Gabe gritted his teeth in a rush of annoyance and anger. Competing for the favor of their father in order to be appointed as successor to the "throne" of the Cress empire was in full swing, changing their family dynamic and pitting the brothers against each other. All to garner their father's approval. And now the goal line had been moved further out of their sights. Gabe was tired of it all, feeling more like a chess pawn than a respected grown man.

He glanced around the table and saw the same sentiments on the faces of his brothers.

This had been their entire life under the rule of Phillip Cress Sr. Firmness. Demands. High expectations. More discipline than softness. As a man, Phillip Sr. was charming. As a husband, he was loving and devoted. As a father, he had been strict. Maybe even manipulating.

The challenge to be named his successor just exposed what had been there all along.

See me? Approve of me? Tell me I'm as good as you. Tell me I'm the best of your sons.

"Now. If we are done, I'd like to bring the meeting to a close," Phillip Sr. said, his deep voice seeming to boom inside the large conference room.

"And just how long are we to remain in this holding pattern while you play with our lives?" Cole asked, ever the rebel.

Gabe envied his boldness.

Phillip Sr.'s jaw visibly tightened.

Nicolette rose with ease and moved to the door to open it. "If the family could have the room, *s'il vous plaît*," she said with a smile meant to soften her clear demand.

As everyone else left, the brothers all rose from their seats and moved about the room as if suddenly uncaged.

"So, you all are upset?" Phillip Sr. asked, remaining in his seat as he eyed each of his sons. "You choose to take umbrage like your brother? The same audacity and disrespect?"

Gabe glanced over at him from his position in front of the floor-to-ceiling window. He frowned when he saw their mother rush to his side and whisper in his ear in French as she pressed kisses to his temple. His parents always had a way of making everyone, including their children at times, feel as if they were intruding on their own little world, one meant just for them.

Most times it was cute. In this moment Gabe found it annoying. His father needed reprimanding not consoling.

"Since everyone is rooting for me to retire and fade to black, as if I have nothing to offer," Phillip Sr. said, pressing a kiss to Nicolette's palm before setting aside her hand and rising from his seat, "why don't each of you tell me why you want to be CEO?"

"I'm the eldest and the most experienced working within the company," Phillip Jr. immediately asserted.

"Sean?" Phillip Sr. asked.

"Honestly?" Sean asked, pausing in pouring himself a glass of Perrier from the bar in the corner. "I'm the star of the company. The most well-known, and my face on the company will only grow the brand."

Gabe turned, assuming he was next by order of age.

"Cole?" Phillip Sr. said.

Surprised by his father's move, he turned back to his view.

"Because you don't think I can do it, and I want to prove you're just as wrong about that as you are about plenty of things," Cole stated.

"Coleman!" Nicolette gasped at his insolence.

"Laisse-le être, bébé," Phillip Sr. said in her native tongue.

Leave him be.

Their father was as used to Cole's shtick as everyone else.

"Lucas?"

"Because you want one of your sons to step in and fill your shoes," Lucas admitted.

"Gabriel?" Phillip Sr. finally called to him.

Again, he looked over his shoulder as he slid his hands into the pockets of his pants. "To grow the company into other culinary markets that will secure the future of Cress, INC. for generations to come," he replied with ease and honesty.

Phillip Sr. nodded and splayed his hands. "And that is why Gabriel would be my top choice were I to step down," he said.

Gabe hated the pleasure that glimmer of approval from his father gave him.

"But imagine my disappointment when you mentioned to your mother and I just last week that you missed being a chef and wished you could find a way to do so in some capacity while still working for Cress, INC. A bunch of nonsense I will *never* support."

Gabe's hand tightened into a fist inside his pocket as he remembered the comment he'd made in passing to his parents. "I also said *in a perfect world*, and trust me, I know this is *far* from that," he said, unable to take the censure from his tone.

Cole chuckled. "Careful, Gabe, you'll lose the top spot and your award for The Perfect Son," he teased.

"Enough, Cole," Phillip Sr. said, his voice low but hard and unbending.

Gabe released a heavy breath, swallowing his own anger as the tension in the room seemed to roar. "But if I'm not guaranteed the position of CEO then why should I—or any of us—alter our lives on the chance of gaining nothing?" he asked.

"Why should I trust the future of the company to someone not willing to make the sacrifice?" Phillip Sr. shot back.

"Because the happiness of your sons should matter," Gabe retorted.

Phillip Sr. threw his hands up in exasperation. "Then be happy and go cook, Gabe, but you cannot have two loves. One will always suffer."

"Good advice, Dad," Cole said suddenly with obvious sarcasm.

Everyone in the room looked at Phillip Sr. and Cole as they shared a long look before Cole turned and strode to the door. "I'm out," he said before leaving.

Gabe had found their brief exchange odd, but barely had time to give it much thought as his father stood and took his mother's hand in his and walked across the conference room, as well. For him, the conversation was not done, but for now, it was clearly over.

He was still annoyed as they all took their leave, but throughout the day, he found it hard to focus on the business proposal to present for board approval for the second CRESS restaurant in Paris.

It was a bitter pill to swallow that his parents held no regard for his happiness.

If nothing else. I've been given the freedom to do as I please and I'm grateful for that.

He lowered his hands from the keyboard and sat back in his chair behind his desk as he remembered the occasion those words had been said to him...

Monica lay on her stomach across the middle of her queen-size bed as Gabe rested on his side beside her with the dark gray satin sheets haphazardly strewn over their lower bodies. He trailed his fingers up and down her spine. He aroused tiny goose bumps across her soft skin as she gazed out the window at the stunning view of darkness claiming the Manhattan heavens as light began to fill windows of the towering skyscrapers in the distance.

The view was as beautiful as her new condo, but neither could rival her beauty when he stroked deep inside her and looked down at the satisfaction in her brown eyes.

They'd enjoyed making fiery love. It had been a week since they'd last sought out each other for pleasure. Although an hour had passed, they lingered in bed, still enjoying each other's presence.

Ding.

He bent to press a kiss to her lower back as she reached to pick up the iPad from the nightstand.

"Room service is on the way," she said, looking back at him over her shoulder.

Monica had purchased a condominium in one of those buildings that was mainly a hotel but had several floors designated for condos, combining the luxury and amenities of a hostelry with home ownership.

Gabe deeply massaged one fleshy cheek of her bottom before giving it a slap. She playfully scowled and arched a brow.

"Just making up for the slap you gave me earlier," he said as she climbed from the bed nude.

He watched her, enjoying the sight of her soft buttocks as she bent over to find her robe, tangled with the duvet strewn on the floor. In the months since they'd become lovers, he'd seen more of her shy facade fade. Nearly gone was the skittish woman who'd made it her business to remain in the background of his family's life. He wasn't sure if it was her sudden wealth and independence or the confidence brought on by knowing he found her his best lover yet—something he had admitted to her on many occasions before, during and after sex.

"Yes, but I wasn't in the right state of mind," she said, pulling on a floor-length white cotton robe that was innocent on a hanger but thrilling on her body.

He loved the way the thin material skimmed her hard nipples and clung to her hips. He was used to lace and silk but found pleasure every time she peeled back her innocence and came alive under his touch. His arousal stirred as she ran her fingers through her disheveled hair and pushed the length behind her shoulders before leaving the room.

Gabe turned to reach for the iPad to turn on the seventy-inch television on the wall above the slate fireplace positioned across from the bed. He flipped through the channels, looking for business news but stopped at the sight of a photo of Monica crossing one of the many busy New York streets. He started to call out to her but stopped, knowing she never talked about the gossip in the press concerning her and her alleged father.

The camera cut to the face of a pretty brown-skinned woman in her seventies with reddish-brown soft curls and a friendly expression who looked very familiar. She and a younger woman were walking the beach as they talked.

"So, Mrs. Maynard, you are confirming the speculation that Monica Darby is in fact your niece by your brother, Brock Maynard?" the entertainment newscaster asked as the woman paused to gaze out at the sun setting above the ocean.

"Absolutely," Phoebe said, resting her hands on her hips. She wore a linen powder blue shirt and pants. "And she may have one of those gag orders stopping her speaking on it, but I don't. I am proud to have her as my niece and just wish we'd had the chance to know each other sooner."

Gabe's mouth opened a bit at that revelation. He moved to rise from the bed and cross the room to stand before the television. It was then he noticed that Monica favored the woman. A lot.

"And do you care to share the real story of her birth?"

"That is a story I will only share with my niece when she is ready to hear it," Phoebe said before turning to give the camera a sparkling smile and a wink Gabe believed to be meant for Monica.

He glanced over and found her paused in the doorway with her hands still gripping the white-linen-covered cart, laden with the food they'd ordered à la carte from the restaurant downstairs.

She moved around the cart to reach the bed and turn off the television with the iPad. "Gabriel," she chided him, facing him with her arms crossed over her chest.

"Why didn't you just say you signed an NDA?" he asked as he retrieved the cart and removed the warmers from the plates.

She arched a brow.

"Right...because you signed an NDA."

She remained silent.

"How are you enjoying your new life?"

"It's more than I ever dreamed of," she admitted, careful with her words.

"But?"

"But you know I can't talk about it...even though I want to," she said. "I want to get out of my own head and process it all, but I can't. So just leave it be. Please."

"Seems like your aunt is more than willing to talk to you. Maybe it's time to take her up on her offer," he said, pulling the sash of her robe and letting it fall

to her sides as he eased one arm around her waist to mold her body against his.

Monica released a grunt of pleasure at the feel of him as she tilted her head back and raised up on the tip of her toes to better enjoy the kisses he pressed to her neck.

"One thing I can say."

Gabe raised his head to look down at her, finding her eyes melancholy.

"If nothing else. I've been given the freedom to do as I please and I'm grateful for that," she admitted.

Gabe didn't allow his recollection to continue on to how he'd scooped her up in his arms and pressed her body beneath his as he helped erase the sadness from her eyes. The empathy he felt sent visceral pains across his chest for her. Somehow Brock Maynard had not spent one day in the life of his daughter, who'd ended up in foster care. It seemed he'd never even spoken of her existence to his lone family member until he was on death's bed.

But he had granted her money to do with as she pleased, to live as she pleased. While his father had been a constant presence in his life but withheld the freedom for him to live his dreams.

Gabe clenched his jaw at the thought of that irony and then he clearly remembered the night at the CRESS restaurant in Paris where he had reconnected with his passion for food. A joy in his life that he'd set aside for the sake of the family business. A sacrifice that was unappreciated by his parents.

Maybe it is time to do as I please and be free...

* * *

"I can't believe you made a scrapbook," Monica said to Phoebe as she flipped through the pages of newspaper clippings and prints of online articles about her.

"*A* scrapbook? I made two. That one's yours," Phoebe said from her seat on the modern sofa as she looked around at the high ceilings, stylish decor and view of Central Park via the floor-to-ceiling windows. "Your apartment is beautiful."

Monica eyed the serviced residence she purchased fully designed and furnished in subtle shades of light gray—it reminded her of the Cress home and had made her love it on first sight when the Realtor had shown it to her. "Sometimes I can't believe it's mine," she said, her voice soft as she stood up and moved about the spacious living room, touching this item and that. Artwork. Fireplace. Soft furnishings. "Everything is so different."

"Are you happy here?" Phoebe asked.

Monica leaned against the doorway of her apartment's Juliet balcony, which overlooked the floral garden of the Midtown Manhattan building. She was still trying to find comfort within her new life. Wealth brought on the expectations that came along with being on the other side of the line separating the haves from the have-nots. Being unemployed with endless time on her hands.

To think.

About the revelation concerning her father.

About the truth telling of her aunt.

About the invasion of paparazzi and gossip reporters upon her privacy.

About the identity of her mother.

And the strong and passionate skill of her lover.

The last made her smile into her glass.

I have a lover.

"Gabe," she whispered into the summer air as her entire body seemed to tingle at the very thought of him.

"What's that you said?" Phoebe asked.

Monica turned with a smile. "I'm happy," she finally answered her.

They saw each other maybe once a week, sometimes every two weeks. No expectations. No dates. No chances of mixed feelings and broken hearts. No fear of being left alone.

Or behind, she thought, thinking of her ex, James.

They knew going into it that the fire would fade and their dalliances would end without either taking offense. It was the perfect way to have Gabe Cress without *having* Gabe Cress. It was their sexy and salacious little secret.

She could only imagine the reaction of his family if they knew—especially his mother. She'd spent five years in their home and had come to know them well. Nicolette Cress was firmly against the mingling of family and staff. Monica doubted her sudden wealth or famous father would change the fact that she would always be Monica the Maid in the woman's eyes. Mrs. Cress would never want to equate a former servant to herself. For *any* reason.

Just hope she doesn't find out about Chef Jillian,

she thought with a hint of spite as she remembered the sexy note she'd stumbled upon in the kitchen.

That made her chuckle.

"All done, Ms. Darby."

Monica turned and eyed one of the building's house-keepers, standing in the living room with her hands locked in front of her in the usual gray uniform dress and comfortable shoes the cleaning staff wore. "Thank you, Olive," she said after reading her name tag.

"You're welcome," she said with a polite nod.

Monica was surprised when the middle-aged woman stopped on her way to the front door and turned.

"Yes?" she asked, feeling more like Nicolette Cress than herself.

It didn't sit well with her.

"I just noticed we never have to actually clean for you. It's always spotless," Olive said, glancing down at her shoes.

Monica knew the show of deference well. Again, she felt ill at ease at her switch in status. "I'm so used to doing it for others, that's all," she said.

"Yes, but if our supervisors were to know, they would assume the housekeeping staff is not doing a good enough job for you," she explained.

Right.

Monica gave her a soft smile. "I understand and I will try to do less," she said, knowing firsthand the security provided by having a job.

Olive said nothing else and continued out the door, quietly closing it behind herself.

Monica gave Phoebe a small smile at the long look her aunt gave her with all-too-knowing eyes.

"Give it time," she said.

"I'm bored out of my mind. There is only so much shopping and spa treatments I can do. I want—*need*—more," she said. "I've always worked. Always. I've never had a choice but to work. Even when I traveled with James, I worked alongside him or took odd jobs as a waitress or cashier to eat up some time before we were on the move to the next location."

"James?" Phoebe asked.

"Ex. Long story."

"I have plenty of those long stories in my seventy years."

"I don't have but the one, and I plan for it to be the only one," she said.

Phoebe chuckled. "Life is too long to believe you will only fall in love once," she advised with a twinkle in her eyes.

"My focus is on starting a business or nonprofit," she asserted. "Not love."

"Doing what, now?"

"I remember the fear and loneliness I felt at aging out of the foster care system and receiving no real financial assistance from the state to start my adult life," she began. "I'm considering asking my attorney, Choice Kingsley, to help me start a nonprofit to help foster care children in the same predicament."

Phoebe's eyes were sympathetic as she eyed her niece. "That sounds like something worth investing some time, and with the rest, you give yourself room to adjust to your new life."

"You'd think after growing up in foster care and learning to adjust to different environments that I'd already know that," Monica said, coming back across the sunlit living room to reclaim her seat on the sofa across from the other woman.

Phoebe's eyes were sad, although she gave her a soft smile. "I would have raised you and loved you if I'd known, but I didn't. I swear I didn't," she said, her voice barely above a whisper.

Monica took a breath. "That's exactly why I called you, to ask the very question of just what do you know?" she said, feeling her stomach twist in knots from fear and anxiousness.

"You're ready now?" Phoebe asked.

Monica sat back against the plush pillows as she crossed one leg over the other and slightly raised one shoulder. "Someone I know suggested it was time," she said, thinking of Gabe.

"Seems like your aunt is more *than willing to talk to you. Maybe it's time to take her up on her offer."*

"This is not easy to say or admit, but it's the truth, and I always say why lie when the truth is sufficient," Phoebe began. "My brother had a taste for younger women. Not teenagers but young. I think they made him relive his glory days while he pretended his hair wasn't turning silver and things below the belt weren't quite as hard as they used to be."

Monica felt a little nervous.

"He met your mother at his favorite twenty-four-hour diner, where she was a waitress."

"How old?" Monica asked.

"Twenty."

"And he was?"

"Forty-two."

She winced. "Was he married?" she asked.

"No, but he and the singer Roz Garnet had an arrangement," Phoebe said. "They met on the set of a movie being made in Hollywood. Whirlwind. She moved back to New York to be with him. Basically gave up her career to have him."

Silly woman in love. Been there. Done that. Not doing it again.

Monica picked up her iPhone from the seat and searched for a photo of the disco singer. She found her to be a mocha-skinned beauty with curly hair and plump lips with her signature shades in place. *She's beautiful.*

"They were together but not together for years, and no one knew. They liked it that way. He left his apartment in Tribeca to her," Phoebe said. "She never had children of her own."

Monica looked up from the phone. "Is that why he didn't want me? To keep from hurting her? Was that my mother's fault? Or mine?" she asked, unable to hide her censure. "And even in his death he protected her from the truth. From me. My existence. It's pretty jacked up."

Phoebe rose and came over to sit beside her niece. "I would never make excuses for my brother's decisions.

I am just giving you the truth," she implored, reaching for Monica's hand to cover with her own.

Monica withdrew it and rose to her feet to put distance between them as she felt the pain of resentment for her father spread across her chest in waves. "And the rest of the truth?" she asked, her voice hollow to her own ears. "My father turned his back on me and hid me so that his lover never felt betrayed. Now, why did my mother? Why did she desert me?"

Phoebe ran her pearl-colored fingertips through her hair as she shifted her gaze away.

"What?" Monica asked, narrowing her eyes as she looked at her.

Phoebe looked down at the floor.

"Why lie when the truth is sufficient?" Monica reminded her.

Phoebe sighed. "Your father admitted to me on his deathbed that your mother couldn't take care of you. She was alone and struggling," she began.

Monica crossed her arms over her chest and hugged herself. Preparing herself.

"He promised her he would raise you but gave you up instead," she admitted with tears in her eyes when she finally locked them with her niece's again.

Monica stiffened her back and knees to keep from swooning at her father's betrayal. It was she who broke their linked eyes as she cast her gaze down to the toes of her crocodile leather flats. "What was her name?" she asked, her voice whisper soft. "What was my mother's name?"

"That, he did not tell me."

She hugged herself tighter and raised her head just as a tear flew down her cheek. "Secrets to the very end, huh?" she asked bitterly.

Phoebe winced and rose to her feet.

Monica shook her head and held up a hand to deny her the right to come closer. She couldn't find any more words. She released a long drawn-out breath between pursed lips as she grappled with yet another loss. "Could you go, please?" she begged, feeling weakened.

"I don't want to go," Phoebe said.

Monica released a bitter laugh. "Welcome to my world. A lot of things I didn't want to happen did," she said with a shrug and a downturn of her lips. "Do like I did and deal with it."

"I know you're angry and hurt. So am I. This man was my brother, and I would have never thought he was capable of turning his back on his own child," Phoebe implored. "I don't agree with him. I think you deserve to be recognized and embraced. That's why I let the world know you were my brother's child and I love you—"

"You don't know me!" Monica yelled, releasing years of frustration and hurt.

"I *know* that you are my niece. You are my blood. And for me…that is enough to love you on sight, Monica Darby," she said with emotion, her eyes wet from her own tears. "You have family. You have me."

Monica swiped her cheek. "You're not my mother, and even now with all the press, she didn't step forward and say *I'm your mother*," she said, drawing a shaky breath.

"But I'm your family," Phoebe insisted, taking a step toward her.

Again, Monica denied her with a shake of her head.

"Okay," Phoebe said, clasping her hands before stepping back and then turning to retrieve her clutch from the sofa where she'd first set it upon her arrival. "I'm going back to Santa Monica tomorrow. My home is your home. Always."

Monica said nothing else as she watched the older woman reluctantly take her leave. The click of the door closing behind her seemed so final. For a moment, she considered running to her aunt and begging her not to go.

Instead, she dried her tears, tucked her pain away, like she'd learned to do as a forgotten foster child, and picked up her iPhone to dial Gabe's number. He answered on the third ring.

"Gabe, I know we just saw each other earlier this week but I need a distraction tonight. Can you help me with that?" she asked.

"You okay?" he asked.

"Nothing you can't make me forget for a little while," Monica said, longing for his presence.

"I'm on the way," he said before ending the call.

By the time she'd showered, brushed down her hair and slipped on a sheer robe, Gabe was at the door. She fell into his arms and captured his lips with her own as soon as he stepped into the foyer. With a deep moan he untied her robe and let it hang open to reveal her nudity before he scooped her body up into his arms with ease and carried her to the bedroom as she clung to him as if starved.

Seven

One month later

Gabe glanced over at Monica dressed in nothing but his tailored shirt as she leaned against the black stone counter watching him cook them dinner. He, on the other hand, wore nothing but a white apron with his buttocks exposed in the back. She gave him a mischievous look as she reached over to swat at one cheek before gripping the hard flesh in her hand as she pressed her chin into his upper arm and looked up at him.

Shit.

He couldn't look away. He felt trapped in her gaze. And when the humor faded from her eyes to be replaced with some other emotion, his gut clenched. It wasn't desire. He knew that look well. She felt more than just an attraction and might expect more from him than just carnal pleasure.

It was something that made him feel an odd mix of excitement and trepidation.

Bzzzzzz.

Thankful for the intrusion, Gabe shifted the pan of seared rib eye steaks from the heat of the Viking stove and picked up his phone from the table. A FaceTime call. "It's Cole. I was supposed to meet up with them for drinks," he said to Monica. He walked out of the kitchen and to the hall before he accepted the connection, being sure to keep his nude body out of the frame.

"What's up, Cole?" Gabe said, looking at his brother and easily recognizing CRESS X's upscale bar setting behind him.

"All your brothers are here. Where are you?" he asked, swiveling the phone to show the Cress men lined up at the copper-topped bar before his frowning face filled the screen again.

"I can't make it," he said, looking into the kitchen to see Monica glance at him before she moved to wash her hands at the rinse sink.

"Yeah, but where are you?" Cole pressed. "And with whom?"

The last thing Gabe wanted was for Monica to become a topic of discussion among his brothers. The fact she was their ex-employee would make the jokes and ribbing all the more raucous. They would assume she had been his in-house lover for the last five years. His instinct was to protect her from that. From gossip. From judgment and speculation. "I'm still at work," he lied, seeing Monica pause in drying her hands with a dish towel. "I'll catch up with y'all at the house later."

"But that's not the off—"

Beep.

Gabe ended the FaceTime call and walked back into the kitchen, setting his phone on the counter. He enjoyed the sight of Monica's smooth legs and the way the hem of his shirt fell just beneath her bottom. When she turned and caught his eyes on her, he didn't look away.

She frowned. "If you had plans, you didn't have to make dinner," Monica said, gripping the edges of the farmhouse-style sink as she leaned back against it.

Gabe used clamps to remove the steaks from the pan and set them on the cutting board to rest. He opened the top oven to remove the tray of root vegetables he'd roasted along with garlic and thyme in an olive-oil-and-lemon mixture. He took his time, thinly slicing the medium-rare steak and plating it before adding a pile of the root vegetables and garnish. Delicious and appealing to the eye.

He set the plate on the island and then poured her a glass of red wine. "I'm exactly where I want to be," he said, handing it to her before pouring himself one, as well, then touched the rim to hers.

Monica was thankful for the shade of the trees as she took her seat on the terrace of the French bistro in the middle of Midtown Manhattan. "I'll have a glass of the house white wine, please," she said to the waiter, opening the tented napkin to lay on her lap across the red wide-leg pants she wore with a matching tank and gold leather flats.

She took a sip of her goblet of ice water as she looked around at the cream-and-brown decor. The terrace was surrounded by six-foot wood panels. Above the panels, the towering skyscrapers surrounded the converted town house housing the restaurant.

She had just begun to peruse the menu when her guest joined her. "Hi, Choice," she said, rising to kiss the woman's smooth brown cheek before they both took their seats across from each other at the bistro table. "Is it hot enough for you?"

Choice Kingsley pushed her shades atop her head and set her crocodile leather briefcase on an empty chair. "Only lunch with you could get me to leave the air-conditioning of my office," she said with a smile.

A junior partner at Curro Villar and Hunt, Choice was recommended to her by Marco Villar to serve as her attorney. A work relationship had slowly become a friendship as Monica found she enjoyed the woman's intelligence and humor. She was easy to talk to and Monica considered her a godsend…and probably the first person she'd truly taken the chance on trusting.

They both ordered quiche lorraine for lunch, with Choice choosing sparkling water with fresh fruit for her drink.

"Business first," Choice said, reaching for her briefcase to remove a black file. "Your 501c3 has been officially established. Congrats on that."

Monica accepted the file and opened it, knowing the certification was only the next step in establishing her charity. It would make any money she collected as a charitable organization exempt from federal taxes. Monica's plan had been to just donate directly from her own money, but Choice had talked her into really making a go of the foundation—solicit funds, set up grants, hire small staff and maybe even a publicist.

"Now pleasure," Choice said, her fork slicing into the egg-and-bacon dish baked in buttery pastry. "How's Gabe? Or better yet how are you and Gabe?"

"Scary," Monica admitted before taking a deep sip of her wine. "We see each other more. Talk more. Call each other more. He cooks dinner. We share things— dreams—with each other. Sometimes we don't even have sex when we meet up. We're breaking all the rules we set—well, all except one. Never to spend any more nights together."

"And that scares you?" Choice asked. "Most women would give up a kidney to have Gabriel Cress in their life in *any* way."

"Most women haven't had their heart broken by both their parents when they were left to grow up in foster care without feeling seen…or loved," she said softly before forcing a sad smile to her lips at the pity in Choice's eyes.

Monica thought of Gabe lying to his brothers about his whereabouts last week and how she'd felt slighted— even though she knew she shouldn't. Somehow that conversation raked up her feelings of self-doubt. Although he was abiding by the perimeters they'd both set, the hurt little girl inside of her felt he was ashamed of his dealings with her and wanted to avoid the disdain his family would feel about him being so closely enmeshed with their former maid.

"Is he seeing anyone else?" Choice asked.

Monica's breath caught.

Is he?

"That's none of my business," she forced herself to say. To truly feel. "If so, she's doing a horrible job keeping him from my door," she added.

"Some men just can't get enough," Choice said.

"The last thing I need is more heartbreak," she said more to herself than Choice.

"You had no control growing up, but you have all of it now," Choice advised.

The waiter refilled her wine and Monica gave him a nod to thank him. "Yes, but the trick is to let my brain stay in control and not my heart," she said.

"Trust me. I agree, friend," Choice said, raising her goblet of fruit-infused water in toast to that.

Two weeks later

Gabe awakened with a start. The room was dark, and it took a moment or two to recognize the tray ceiling of his bedroom. He sat up in the middle of the bed and wiped his eyes with his hands as he yawned.

The sound of light snores caused him to freeze. He leaned over left and then right to check on the floor beside the bed. He raised the covers and lifted the pillows. There sat his iPhone, still on speaker with Monica's name across the top. He chuckled as he picked it up.

They'd been talking late into the night and had fallen asleep. Something he hadn't done since high school.

He frowned and ended the call, staring off into the distance and not really seeing anything.

Monica had happened to call him to ask for advice about her nonprofit at a time when he'd been frustrated by yet another argument between two of his brothers. He revealed to her that the competitiveness in his family was tedious to him and that he desired to reconnect with his love of cooking. He was now curious why he felt the desire to share these things with her.

She had encouraged him to find a balance. To be happy with his life's decisions. Live with no regrets. Treasure his family. That exchange between them had been natural. Comfortable.

The very idea of that growing ease between them caused him to wrinkle his brow and tumble deep into his thoughts as he turned his head to look out the crack in his curtains at the streetlight outside.

Ding.

Gabe removed the glasses he used for reading and set his book down on the sofa as Monica lifted her feet from his lap so he could rise and walk over to the door. He soon returned with a tray, carrying the carafe of coffee and croissants they'd ordered. He set it down on the leather ottoman before pouring her cup first and adding the creamer and four packets of sugar she always favored.

Monica set aside the folders of materials she was reviewing of office spaces and clerical staff for her nonprofit, which she had yet to name. In turn, she added a thin layer of butter to two croissants just the way she had come to learn he enjoyed them. Moving almost in a rhythm, she handed him the croissants and took the cup of coffee he offered her. She took a deep sip of the steaming light and sweet brew.

He slid his reading glasses back on and smiled as he took a bite of the buttery pastry before taking a sip of his own black coffee. He'd come over for a lunch-time tryst that had extended to a leisurely afternoon on her sofa. Raising his arms, she slid her feet back on his lap, and without a word spoken, they both enjoyed their snack and got lost in their reading.

One week later

"My mother caught one of my brother's overnight companions in the house," Gabe said from his seat across from her at her glass dining room table.

Monica took a bite of the spinach, sausage and homemade egg pasta in garlic-tomato sauce he'd made for dinner. "Let me guess? Lucas," she said, around the food.

Gabe chuckled. "Right," he said. "Ever since the weight loss, he has been enjoying the extra attention the ladies give him."

"What did she do?" Monica asked after a sip of white wine.

Nicolette Cress was all about things being done appropriately. The facade of the Cress family and their empire always had to be of a certain caliber.

"She politely escorted the young lady and Luc to the door," Gabe said.

"*And* Luc?" Monica asked in surprise.

He nodded. "And then she proceeded to wake up the entire household and go on a ten-minute tirade about respect, decorum, decent women and gentlemen, and how none of those things were to be found in the Cress family home that night."

"But Lucas missed the speech," she pointed out.

"That was about three in the morning," Gabe said, picking up the bottle of wine to refill both their glasses. "We all heard it again at breakfast when he returned."

"Three?" Monica asked with a wince.

"You think the new housekeeper heard all the ruckus?" he asked.

"Absolutely. The vents carry plenty of juicy details," she advised him with a playful wink.

She thought of Chef Jillian's note and started to share it with him but refrained, keeping that and other endless secrets she held about the family. First, she felt it wasn't her place. Second, she'd signed an NDA. Third, she felt it would only make the strained nature of the family much worse.

Like the surveillance reports I saw in the Cresses' bedroom.

"Sometimes I forget you…"

She arched a brow as his words trailed off. "That I was the family's maid?" she offered. "Trust me, I haven't."

He set his glass and fork down as he sat back in his chair to look across the table at her. "Do you regret it?"

"Working for a living? Never," she asserted, claiming her pride in her work as a maid.

Bzzzzzz.

Monica used the hand not clutching her glass to turn her phone over on the table where it sat. She recognized the number. Bobbie Barnett.

Answer it.

"Damn," she swore.

"What's wrong?"

She shifted her gaze over to Gabe. "Two weeks ago, I hired a private investigator to find the identity of my mother," she admitted, feeling her heart pound with the force of a sledgehammer. "That's her calling."

Bzzzzzz.

His eyes locked on the phone. "Answer it," he said, as he shifted his gaze back to hers.

Strengthened by his presence, she picked up the phone and answered the call as she pushed back her chair before rising. "Hello," she said, moving across the kitchen and living room of the open area to reach the window showcasing Manhattan at night.

As she listened to the PI, the emotion in her eyes shifted in the glass's reflection, moving from fear and slight excitement to shock. Grief. Sadness. And finally they went dull as she felt a chill race over her form.

Monica closed her eyes and released short gasps as her hand tightly gripped the phone.

"Ms. Darby? Are you still there?" Bobbie said.

Monica nodded, but then remembered the woman could not see her. "Yes," she said, her voice sounding hollow to her own ears.

"I just emailed my report to you, and please let me know if there's anything I can help you with in the future."

Anger rose quickly. Irrationally. She knew it and clung to it because anything was better than yet another disappointment. "Crappy time to strike up new business, isn't it?" she asked, her tone clipped and rigid.

"Ms. Darby, I meant no harm and I am so sorry for your loss," she said, her voice soft.

Loss? Losses was more like it.

Monica ended the call and let the phone carelessly drop to the floor as she allowed the full weight and meaning of her mother's death just a year ago settle around her. Engulf her. Take her back to a time when loss was common. It all just seemed cruel. And when tears dared to well up and pain radiated across her chest, Monica used a trick from childhood to go numb. Not feel. Not let her emotions weaken her.

"Damn," she swore again, feeling her childhood trick fail.

She wrapped her arms around herself as she leaned her head against the window.

My mother and father are dead.

The hope of her inner child—the one she fought so hard to ignore—faded like a candle. For years she'd hoped they would return and reclaim her. They never had.

They never will now.

That stung.

I will never know them.

She winced and closed her eyes.

Just as I opened up to every hope of having her in my life...

One tear fell. Loss after loss after loss after loss. Like dominoes.

Father God.

"Monica? What's wrong?"

She opened her eyes and looked over at him standing across the room. Gabriel Cress. Handsome. Talented. Wealthy. Sexy. Wanted.

She cringed and closed her eyes as she held herself tighter. In that moment all she saw was someone else she would lose. "My mother died last year," she said, fighting the urge to release a long wail and give voice to the varied emotions swirling inside her.

Drowning her.

The abandonment and now the loss. Again.

And the cry came. Like a roar. Seeming to be torn from her. Echoing up to the high ceilings and bouncing off the walls. Gabe rushed to her side and turned her to pull her body close to his as he wrapped his strong arms around her. One hand massaged her neck beneath the layers of her hair and the other pressed against her back.

"Let it out. I got you. I'm here," he said into her ear. "I got you."

But for how long?

Monica buried her face against his neck and allowed herself for a moment to imagine it was forever. That he could want her in his life and not just in his bed. That she could live without fear of being hurt.

She pressed a kiss to his neck and closed her eyes

to inhale deeply of his warm and familiar scent as she accepted what she had been ignoring all along. She had come to rely on him. Expect him. Miss him.

And if things did not end, she would come to love him. And then lose him.

Fear made her freeze in his arms.

She couldn't take one more loss.

"You are the last thing I need and everything I need at this moment," Monica admitted in a soft voice as she forced her body to relax as she clung to him and freed herself of him all at once.

When she felt Gabe step back from her, she took a steadying breath and looked up into his handsome face, forcing herself to do what needed to be done. "Gabe, it's over. This thing between us. It's time. It's over. It's done," she said, moving away from him.

He frowned. "What? Why?" he asked, stepping toward her.

She shook her head and held up her hands. "I'm ending it before you do," she said. "Before I get hurt. Before I lean on you and depend on you and get used to you any more than I already have."

Gabe slid his hands into his slacks and stood rigid as he eyed her for the longest time. "So, I'm the bad guy?" he asked.

"Am I wrong?" she countered.

He looked down at his feet as he clenched and unclenched his jaw. The moments seemed to tick by ever so slowly. "We both agreed that whenever one of us said it was done then it was done," he said.

"Right," Monica said, fighting the urge to run to him and be wrapped in his arms again.

Gabe looked up and locked his eyes on her. "This is what you want?" he asked, his voice deep and serious and final.

There in the depths was an ultimatum. She knew her answer would lead to him walking out the door and never returning.

"Yes," she lied before turning her back on him and closing her eyes as she fought to do what she knew needed to be done to save herself any more heartbreak.

Monica stood by the fireplace and gripped the mantel. She listened as he gathered his suit jacket, tie, briefcase and keys, and then his footsteps echoed against the wood floors as he walked to the door and opened it. Like a fool she dared to glance back over her shoulder and saw him paused in the open doorway with his back to her. He turned his head and showed his profile. His jaw was rigid.

"I am deeply sorry about your mother," he said. "If there is ever *anything* I can do for you to help you, just ask, and I'll get it done."

She believed him. That was the problem. He was so very easy to love.

She looked away from him.

Moments later the door softly closed behind him.

Monica released the mantel and allowed her knees to go out beneath her. There, atop the plush area rug, she curled her body into the fetal position and wept. For the mother she would never know. The father who'd abandoned her. And the love she was afraid to have.

Another loss.
At least this time it was my choice.

One month later

Gabe left the bathroom of his parents' eight-bedroom country estate in the village of Saint-Germain-en-Laye, twenty miles outside Paris, with a towel draped around his waist and another over his head as he dried his hair. Letting the damp cloth fall to his shoulders, he walked over to the large windows and looked out at the beauty of the countryside. The sun was just beginning to set and the skies were painted in dreamy colors as day shifted to night. A wind blew across the fields and sent wildflowers swaying back and forth among the emerald grass. In the distance were the red roofs of the homes in the village. Trees with leaves in shades of green, gold and claret towered, offering shade and some relief from the heat.

With approval from the board of Cress, INC., Gabe had been in Paris the last month overseeing the construction and launch of CRESS XI. At times the solace of the large country estate was haunting, but most days, he was glad to be free of the continuing rivalry among his brothers. And the work kept him busy and his thoughts occupied.

He wished he had more control as he slept. His dreams of her betrayed him.

Bzzzzzz.

He looked back over his shoulder at his iPhone on the pine French-provincial dresser. He strode across the room to flip it over and accepted the disappointment he felt that it wasn't *her* calling.

So be it.

He wouldn't be the one to make the first move. And perhaps it was for the best. What future could they have? She lacked trust and he thrived on ambition. Neither was equipped for more between them.

Eight

One week later

Monica lowered the rear window from her position on the back seat of the all-black SUV with dark tinted windows. "Gabe," she called over to him once the vehicle he exited drove away and revealed him standing on the street.

Her heart raced at the very sight of him. His shortbread complexion seemed darker. His beard fuller. His body a bit more fit in the navy long-sleeved tee and dark denims he wore with cognac oxford sneakers.

He turned in surprise and looked up and down the length of the street before he finally noticed her in the SUV parked at the curb a few houses down from the Cress townhome. He smiled and it transformed his face.

Her heart raced and her entire body went warm.

The last month without him had proven nothing except that her feelings for Gabe ran beyond just the physical. Against her better instincts and rational thought. She was hooked. She couldn't turn him loose.

Monica motioned for him to come to her before raising the window and disappearing behind the darkness of the glass. Her eyes stayed locked on him as he strode across the street. Her entire body felt like a bundle of nerves. There was happiness to see him. Desire to have him. But also fear.

She pushed the latter away as he opened the rear door.

"I am not ready to say goodbye to you forever, Gabe," she admitted, feeling as if the moment was all or nothing.

He eyed her with such intensity.

Time slowed.

She licked at her lips, feeling as if they were suddenly dry.

His eyes dropped to take in the move she'd made in all innocence.

She gasped when he locked his gaze on hers and extended his hand. She looked down at it and then up at him before sliding hers into his.

"Get out," he said, his voice deep.

It sounded so good to her ears.

He helped her exit the car. As soon as her feet touched on the ground, he pulled her body close to his and lowered his head to hers.

Her alarmed eyes looked past his shoulder to the family's home. "What if someone sees us?" she whispered in a panic.

"I don't care."

And there, pressed against the side of the vehicle, they kissed with every bit of the hunger they felt for each other, with panting breaths and excitement beyond measure.

"What are we doing, Gabe?" she asked in between electric kisses.

He raised her chin with his finger to look into her eyes. "Taking a chance on each other."

Monica released a grunt of pleasure as she wiggled her body back against Gabe's warmth as he spooned her from behind. She had to admit that the nights he stayed over were the best. It had been a long time since she'd slept with someone, and even then, nothing compared to the security she felt from Gabe's arm stretched over her waist and one of his feet lightly resting atop hers as they slumbered. It had been only two weeks since his return from Paris, and the nights he wasn't with her, she felt his loss.

Her fear rose, but she pushed it down deep as she felt the warmth of his kisses against her shoulder. She raised her arm to stroke the back of his head before lifting her hair to expose her nape to him. He pressed a kiss there without fail, evoking a shiver. It was a sensitive spot that he'd discovered and exploited.

Monica lay on her back to look up at him. Giving

him a smile, she stroked his face. "I'm glad you got rid of the beard," she said. "The shadow is much better."

He grabbed the rim of the sheet and flung it back from her body. "I like yours, too," he mused, looking down at the thin layer of soft hairs covering the plump vee.

Arching a brow, she grabbed the side of the sheet covering him and flung it toward the foot of the bed. She took in his nudity before surrounding his inches with her hand. "You could use a trim," she said, lightly playing in the soft curly bush surrounding his thick member.

Gabe chuckled. "You weren't complaining last night," he reminded her.

Monica flushed in embarrassment and playfully nudged his side with her knuckles. "Careful. Brag about it and it might be the last," she warned.

"If you cut me off, then I'll do the same," he said, palming her intimately as he bit his bottom lip.

"Touché," she said playfully, enjoying their banter.

Gabe held her body and rolled them together until she was under him. "A quick shower and we both could be happy…and at the same time," he said with twinkling eyes before dipping his head to nuzzle her neck.

Her fingers gripped his shoulders. "Shower together, okay," she said. "I still have to get an outfit for your parents' cocktail party tonight."

"Don't stress it. You're always gorgeous," he said, sliding one hand beneath her to cup one soft and fleshy buttock.

Monica gave him an indulgent smile as she stroked

his jawline with her thumb. "How about we discuss how bad of an idea me attending this party is?" she said sweetly.

Gabe released a low grunt and shook his head. "I thought we debated this enough last night," he said, releasing her to sit on the bed.

She rose and retrieved her robe from the chair where he'd knelt before her and spread her knees wide to feast. They'd enjoyed dinner at CRESS X and then she'd served up dessert.

"New day. New debate," she said as she tied the robe and turned to face him as she pulled her hair up into a messy topknot.

Gabe shifted to sit back against the headboard with his legs outstretched and crossed at the ankle. He splayed his hands and dipped his head a little as if to say "bring it."

Monica crossed her arms over her chest and bit back a smile. "Why do you want this?" she asked.

"Because I want you in my life, and there is no need to keep it from my family," he said.

"Anymore," she added.

"Anymore," he agreed.

She fell silent as she crossed the floor to stand before the windows. Monica had been witness to the Cress soirees for their family and wealthy friends. And never had she yearned to attend as a guest. Pretending she belonged.

The pretense. The facade.

The bull—

"What else, Monica?" he asked, interrupting her thoughts.

"What exactly did you tell your parents?" she asked.

"They know I am bringing a guest," he replied.

She glanced back over her shoulder. "Me?"

"No," he admitted.

"This will not end well, Gabe," she advised, shifting her gaze back out the window.

She was not surprised when he walked up behind her to wrap his arms securely around her. She leaned back against his strength.

"What's the worst that could happen?" he asked as he lightly settled his chin atop her head.

"One of them tries to kill me," she said.

"Realistically," he asserted.

She locked her eyes on his reflection in the glass. "They throw me out," she said.

"My mother? Ms. Decorum?" he mused with the hint of laughter.

"Okay…she'll politely escort me to the front door and then wish me a good evening before softly closing the door in my face with a smile," she said.

"Now that sounds about right," he said. "Raquel did not see my mother's show of real emotion until after the wedding, and she dated Phillip Jr. for three years."

"Hell, I lived with you all for five years and rarely saw it, but if you pay close attention, she has telltale signs about how she really feels," she said.

"Like the death grip on some item while she smiles at you," he offered.

She nodded. *"Exactly,"* she stressed.

Gabe dipped his head to press a kiss to her temple before he turned her to face him. "Come with me tonight just because I want to be able to look across the room and see you there," he said in a low voice. "And there is nothing *anyone* can say or do to make me regret having you there with me."

She raised up on the tip of her toes to rub her cheek against his before taking his hand in hers and leading him to the bathroom to shower *and* pleasure each other.

But her fears and mild anxiety on the upcoming event remained right there on the surface. She couldn't ignore it. Not as they enjoyed breakfast or traveled to look at a small office in a converted warehouse in Brooklyn that she was considering using for her foundation. Nor when they enjoyed a light dinner at a restaurant before going back to her apartment to get dressed. Even up to the moment their hired car service pulled up in front of the town house.

As Gabe helped her from the rear of the SUV and she looked up at the impressive structure with its intricate detailing, she searched inside herself to see if in hindsight she had been happy during her time working there. She had. With the job had come a stability she had never known before.

"Ready?"

Monica glanced over at Gabe and then looked down at the long-sleeved silk chiffon dress she wore. With its plunging neckline, a dreamy dusty rose-and-cream print design and short flounced hem, she felt beautiful and sexy. The cut fit her small breasts and curvy hips well. "How do I look?" she asked.

"Perfect," he assured her, raising her hand in his to press a kiss to the back.

"Good," she said.

The front door opened and Cole stepped out onto the porch in an all-navy suit and tie. "I'll be there in twenty minutes," he said on his phone before ending the call.

Monica felt so nervous that she focused on each step they took, careful not to stumble in her four-inch strappy heels.

"Hello, stranger," Cole said as he reached for a gold case from his inside pocket and placed a cigar between his teeth.

"I just saw you the night before last," Gabe reminded him as they briefly tapped fists in greeting.

Cole's gaze shifted to Monica. He did a double take and then his eyes widened in surprise before dipping to take in their entwined hands. "Money and getting away from this family—well, most of us—has done you good," he said.

"Hello, Cole," she said.

He inclined his head in greeting as he smiled, then he turned and opened the front door.

"I thought you were leaving?" Gabe asked as they joined him on the top step.

"And miss Mama slip into full Stepford Wife mode? No. *This* should be fun," he said as they stepped into the marble foyer.

Gabe held her hand a little tighter.

Monica took a deep steadying breath. "No worries. I got this," she said, hoping she truly did. "Fortunately, foster care taught me how to adapt to new situations."

Delicate piano music mingling with the conversation of those in attendance welcomed them once they stepped into the living room.

"Good luck, kiddo," Cole said to her before moving past them to claim a drink from the bar.

There were about fifty people scattered about the room with drinks in hands and fashion on display. Monica recognized many of them. And as the chatter began to die down, she realized they also recognized her—whether from her work as the Cress maid or from seeing her image exploited by the paparazzi. Either way, the stares and the looks of surprise were disconcerting.

Gabe took a step forward, but Monica felt rooted in place. He stroked her skin with his thumb, and she forced herself to move alongside him toward where his parents stood before the grand fireplace. Phillip's frown was clear and Nicolette's grip on her flute was tight enough for the skin covering her knuckles to thin.

Here we go.

"Gabriel and Monica, you're finally here," Nicolette said, with an artificially bright smile as she waved them over with her free hand.

Oh, she's quick.

Monica did not miss that she whispered something in Phillip Sr.'s ear that led him to try his best to flip his frown. His failed attempt was *almost* comical.

The chatter resumed, but they were aware all eyes were on them as they reached the couple.

Gabe freed her as he pressed a kiss to his mother's cheek and extended his hand to his father, giving him a hard stare daring him to ignore it. "You both remember Monica?" he said.

"Of course," Phillip Sr. said, leaning in to deliver an air-kiss to her cheek. "You look stunning."

"Hello, Mr. and Mrs. Cress," Monica said, hearing her own nervousness. "And you look beautiful as always."

And she did. Nicolette's rose-gold metallic dress fit her tanned skin and dusty-blond hair streaked with silver.

But beyond the beauty, in the depths of her blue eyes, Monica saw her annoyance. Her anger. Her shock. Behind the smile a million questions were flying through the woman's head. All of the who, what, where, when, and perhaps most important, why.

Of that Monica was sure. She notched her chin a little higher, pulling from the toughness she'd developed as a foster kid. *I got this*, she reassured herself.

Nicolette took in the subtle move and smiled before giving Gabe a look that promised him there was more to come later. "Enjoy yourselves," she said, wrapping her arm around her husband's to guide him away.

"Your mother deserves an Oscar," she said.

Gabe laughed. "And my father looks like he needs an enema."

"Absolutely," Monica agreed.

He faced her and reclaimed her hand.

"Everyone is staring," she whispered up to him.

"That's because you're so beautiful," he said, stroking her inner palm with his thumb.

Then why did it take you five years to see me?

"Champagne?"

Monica looked at a middle-aged woman in a gray uniform holding a tray of champagne-filled flutes. "No, thank you," she said with a warm smile.

She felt uncomfortable being served when she used to be the one doing the serving. She remembered all too well how much she hated that part of her job. She didn't doubt the Cresses' new housekeeper felt the same.

"Thank you, Felice," Gabe said as he took a flute from the tray.

"Yes, thank you, Felice," Monica said, being sure to look the woman in the eye and acknowledge her more than she'd ever been in the same scenario.

"You're welcome," Felice said with a nod and smile before moving on.

"You want something else to drink?" Gabe asked.

"Actually," she began, before reaching to take his flute and enjoy a full sip, "you know I—"

"—love champagne," they finished in unison.

But then Gabe frowned in obvious confusion over why she hadn't just taken a flute from Felice.

Monica looked about the room over the rim of the glass. Phillip Jr. and Raquel looked away when her eyes landed on them. Lucas sat beside the pianist, his eyes closed, swaying back and forth to an upbeat rendition of "You Are So Beautiful." A pair of women whose names she chose to forget but whose pretentious faces were etched into her brain gave her odd looks. She responded with a high eyebrow raise. Sean was in the center of a small crowd who looked at him in slight rapture as he spoke. And Cole, still sitting on the steps, raised his snifter of brown liquor in a toast to her, making her smile.

Felice walked up to them carrying a tray of heavy hors d'oeuvres.

Again, Monica politely declined, earning her a brief, odd look from the housekeeper.

"Mr. Cress, your father would like you and your brothers to join him in the study," she said.

Gabe nodded. "Thank you, Felice."

With one last quick look at Monica, the woman moved on about the room, offering the guests the decadent appetizers and informing each brother of their father's request.

"A family meeting midparty?" Monica asked. "I think my nose will be itching."

Gabe pressed his hand to her lower back and she felt the heat of his touch through the thin material. "Honestly? That's probably true."

She smiled to shield her nervousness as she straightened his silk tie before smoothing her hands across the lapels of his suit. "Don't get spanked?" she lightly teased.

"And you take nothing off *anyone*," Gabe stressed.

"You're leaving me alone in the wild?" she said.

"I'll keep you company."

They both turned to find Raquel standing beside them. Phillip Jr. continued on to the stairs, where he patted Cole's shoulder on his way past him.

"Thanks, Raq," Gabe said before striding away, as well, to follow his brothers up the stairs.

"Interesting," Raquel said, raising her flute of champagne in a toast to her. "You absolutely just made my night."

"Did I?" Monica asked before enjoying another sip.

"Sometimes it's nice to see the facade of Nicolette crack just a little," she admitted. "And tonight, she is barely holding it together."

Monica eyed the woman of whom they spoke and wholeheartedly agreed. It would be clear only to those who really knew Madame Cress that the constant touches to her hair, biting at her lips, gripping of everything she touched and movement about the room revealed she was livid and probably fully in favor of her husband lambasting Gabe.

Yes. It was amusing to watch her fight like hell to keep it together.

Monica smiled into her glass.

"Shall we kill one of the elephants in the room?" Raquel asked. "Before or after?"

Monica was no fool. The woman wanted to know if her dealings with Gabe started before or after she ended working for the family. She was clear it was none of Raquel's business—or anyone else's. Her days of obligation to the Cress family were over. "After," she lied.

"Mama, I want to come to the party!"

Monica looked up at Phillip Jr. and Raquel's daughter, Collette, standing at the top of the stairs in a shiny pink dress, a pair of her mother's heels and red lipstick smeared haphazardly around her mouth.

"Oh! All dressed for the party," she said, as everyone in attendance began to laugh.

"Let her come to the party, Raq," a woman in the crowd yelled.

"Yes, let her come to the party," someone agreed.

"Definitely not," Raquel said, handing her flute to a passing server before quickly crossing the room and taking the stairs to gather Collette's hand in her own and guide her back up to her room.

Left alone and feeling watched, Monica moved through the crowd scattered about the spacious living room to the kitchen. Jillian was wiping her hands with a small towel that she then flung over her left shoulder before wiping her sweaty brow with her arm.

Monica tapped the side of her glass with the oversize gold ring on her index finger. "Kudos, Chef," she said.

Jillian smiled in surprise. "What are you doing here?" she asked as she took in Monica's dress and new flowing waves of her hair. "Are you a guest?"

"Of Gabriel's," Monica admitted.

Jillian looked surprised, then pleased and then curious.

"Before. Once," she said, giving her the truthful answer to the elephant found in yet another room. "Lots. After."

Jillian fell silent and lightly touched her chin as she looked off in the distance.

Monica thought of the note one of the Cress family members had left for her: *the taste of you still lingers on my tongue.*

Maybe even Gabriel.

"Penny for your thoughts?" Monica said, coming into the kitchen to stand on the other side of the island.

The women eyed each other.

Jillian smiled. It was a little sad. Melancholy. "Lots. During," she admitted. "After I quit one day? None."

She understood that Jillian had just admitted to her own delicious dalliances with one of the Cress men.

"Who?" Monica asked, ready for her curiosity about the note to end.

"*Not* Gabe," Jillian assured.

"Fair enough," Monica said.

Jillian laughed a bit and turned to pull trays from both double ovens.

"Why does it have to end after you stop working here?" Monica asked.

"Different reasons," Jillian said, using silicone tongs to plate the trays of stuffed puff pastry. "Mostly because I don't think he will ever see me as anything but the cook."

Monica leaned against the edge of the island and turned her head to look down the length of the kitchen and dining room to the backyard. The sight of the illuminated water feature was soothing in that moment as her own fears surfaced. "So, can Gabe see me as more than a maid?" she asked softly, wishing she was outdoors and could hear the sound of the running water.

"It's different," Jillian said. "Money changes *everything*."

Monica looked down at the pastries. They looked delicious. "May I? I'm hungry," she said.

At that moment, Felice entered the kitchen and set her empty serving tray on the island. "Mrs. Cress would like more of the roast beef sliders," she said, her voice stiff. "Perhaps you should offer the lady one before you place them on my tray."

Monica could see the woman was offended. "Felice, I was the Cress maid before you—"

"I know. You're the talk of the party," the woman said.

"I'm sure I am," Monica said dryly.

"I *know* you are," Felice countered. "It's hard to miss when you're moving from crowd to crowd overhearing them."

"What are they saying?" Monica asked, hating that she even cared.

Jillian and Felice shared a brief look that gave the housekeeper the okay to repeat the things she couldn't help but overhear.

"They ridiculed Mr. Cress for openly dating the help," she said with reluctance.

"I'd bet good money *they* were the socialites scowling at me," Monica said, feeling annoyance.

Felice remained silent. Her reticence with Monica was clear.

"Listen, the part of the job I hated the most was serving food at parties," Monica continued, needing to explain herself to the woman. "I didn't take the food because I remember being in your position and hating it so much. I'm not comfortable being served. That's all."

Felice's face softened. "In that moment it felt like you thought my touch was dirty," she said.

"Never," Monica stressed, reaching to touch the woman's hand.

"If you are gonna move in the company of the haves

then it's gonna be hard to keep the mindset of the have-nots," Felice said.

Translation: Do I belong out there with the guests or in the kitchen with the staff?

She knew where she felt most comfortable.

Felice used tongs to set an array of hors d'oeuvres on a saucer and handed it to Monica. "And you didn't hear it from me, and I will deny if asked, but that little gathering upstairs is *all* about you," she said before taking the tray of treats out to the guests.

As Jillian went back to cooking, Monica enjoyed a slider and eyed the elevator. She wiped her fingertips with a napkin and checked to make sure no one in the living room noticed when she made her way toward it. As she took it one flight up to the second floor, she *almost* convinced herself she had every right to hear what was being said about her. Knowing the elevator opened up directly into the master bedroom of Nicolette and Phillip Sr., she continued up to the third floor via the stairs, careful to make sure the double doors leading into the suite of rooms was closed.

"Is *she* the reason for your insanity lately?"

Monica winced as Phillip Sr.'s deep and gravelly voice echoed through the wood. She moved closer to the door and prayed no one stormed out and caught her.

"She's the reason I'm happy," Gabe returned.

Aw. Same.

"Happy or horny?"

"Both."

Someone laughed and Monica just *knew* it was Cole.

Silence reigned and Monica wondered what was going on that she could not see.

"There are women you wed and those you bed. Know the difference. And that goes for all of you," Phillip Sr. said.

"Don't disrespect her in that way," Gabe said, his voice hard and his anger clear. "I tolerate a lot from you, but I will not put up with that—"

"Tolerate!"

Monica jumped, feeling as if Phillip Sr.'s voice booming against the walls was enough to rattle the entire house. She moved from the door and hurried down the stairs, not wanting to hear any more. Wishing she hadn't dared to hear any of it at all.

On the second floor, she paused and pressed her back against the wall as she struggled to slow and steady her breath. Looked down upon by his friends. Judged by Nicolette. Insulted by Phillip Sr. Defended by Gabriel.

The latter made her smile.

She made her way back to the kitchen via the elevator and tried not to let her fears be exploited by her current company. But as she reentered the living room and claimed a new flute from a tray Felice carried around the room, she felt on display.

"Chin up," Felice advised.

They shared a smile.

"Aw, the new maid and the old maid have a little moment."

Monica stiffened before she turned to find one of the socialites standing behind her. She missed not one cliché detail, from her hair to her designer clothing. Those things were clearly her armor. She just wondered what the woman was hiding behind them. Possibly insecurity? That thought led to Monica giving her a pitying smile.

The young woman's face tightened in anger. "Could you fetch me a dirty martini?" she asked, her tone mocking.

Monica wasn't sure of the reason for the woman's anger with her and was bored by it and her. She took a sip of her champagne as she turned to take her leave. She gasped to find Gabe standing beside her. He pressed a reassuring hand to the middle of her back, and she felt as if he'd pushed a battery into it and given her new life.

Take nothing off anyone.

"Thank God, you're back," she said, turning to face the woman who had appointed herself her nemesis. "Suddenly the air is less vile."

The woman stiffened and released a harsh gasp.

Gabe pierced her with his grayish-blue eyes. "Go play your games elsewhere, Naomi," he warned in a cold voice.

Even Monica was chilled by it. She felt relief, like a schoolchild saved from a bully, as the woman clenched both her jaw and the crystal flute of champagne before walking away.

"I don't belong here, Gabe," Monica said, taking a deep sip of her drink in hopes of easing her insecurities.

The behavior of his family and friends was proof

that money could not buy respect. To them she was still the maid in expensive dress-up.

"I'm here and you belong with me," he said.

In his eyes she found the strength she needed. Being with Gabe meant merging their worlds and taking whatever came along with it—to a degree.

"How was the meeting?" she asked.

The light in his eyes dimmed a little. "Enlightening," he said.

"Care to share?"

He forced a smile that did not reach his eyes as he shook his head. "Not yet."

Monica reached for one of his hands and started playfully swaying back and forth as she made little silly expressions meant to lift his spirits.

He gave her a reluctant chuckle before pulling her close for a hug as he pressed a warm kiss to her neck. "Let's go," he said.

"Where?"

"You came here with me, and now I'll go wherever you lead."

Monica leaned back to look up at him. "Anywhere?" she asked.

"Anywhere," he promised.

Cloaked by darkness, Gabriel leaned against the doorway to their private overwater bungalow at the Four Seasons Resort Bora Bora. He glanced back over his shoulder at Monica, asleep in the middle of the king-size bed, before facing forward and resting his gaze on the dark shadow of Mount Otemanu in the distance.

He needed the quiet and had been unable to sleep even though they'd left for their trip just a few hours after they'd ducked out of the cocktail party.

During their thirteen-hour flight, mini-chaos had reigned. Photos of them together at the cocktail party had been leaked to the press. Their relationship had become gossip fodder. The tale of a former maid, who was the secret love child of a former Hollywood star, now dating a member of the family she used to work for, seemed too salacious to be ignored. Particularly with the speculation of just when their relationship had begun.

His phone was ceaselessly ringing with calls from his family members, but he ignored them all. His disconnect from them had begun before the scandal that brought the Cress, INC. brand into the fray.

"There are women you wed and those you bed. Know the difference."

His anger at Phillip Sr.'s words rose as if he'd just heard them for the first time. He was offended by the insult, and such a mindset disturbed him—particularly coming from his father. His respect and admiration of his father's talent, wisdom and profound love for their mother had been immense. Those traits he admired were suspect with the things he'd said in that meeting. Gabe was questioning if they were different men at their core and why he'd fought so hard for his father's hard-earned approval.

He decided it was time to take his own advice.

Take nothing from anyone.

And in the silence, the answer he searched for came

to him. The idea was not new, just something he had been hesitant to accept. But now he was sure.

It was time to walk away from Cress, INC. and open his own restaurant.

With one last look at the moonlight upon the lagoon, he turned and crossed the bedroom to reclaim his place in bed beside his woman. With his decision made, and feeling inspired by her strength, resilience and her kindness, even with the tough times life had tossed upon her, he wrapped his arm over her waist and finally was able to join her in sleep.

Nine

Two months later

Monica came to a stop in the hall before the frosted glass door. She reached out and lightly touched the words etched out in the film. "The Bridge," she read aloud, remembering Gabe helping her to finally choose a name for her foundation when she expressed wanting to fill the gap between childhood in foster care and adulthood alone.

And now, with the use of her inheritance, she had a small office space in a three-story building in the Dumbo section of Brooklyn and was about to walk inside and greet her small staff.

Just another new beginning. That's all. You got this, she thought to herself.

Monica worked her shoulders in the fitted jewel-neck, long-sleeved lace shirt she wore over lightweight tweed high-rise trousers with flared legs. She reached for the door knob. "Wait," she said, reaching inside her crocodile leather briefcase for her oversize tortoiseshell readers to slide on. With her sleek ponytail, she hoped they made her look older, more serious and smart.

She opened the door and stepped inside. Four women turned to view her from where they stood in the center of the large room, its four desks situated two on each side, facing each other.

"Good morning," she said, setting her purse and briefcase on one of the six waiting room chairs before moving over to each person: her two full-time employees, Kylie Branch, her administrative assistant, and Nylah Hunt, her grant writer and chief financial officer. Choice, volunteering to serve pro bono as chief counsel. And Montgomery Morgan, her on-call publicist.

She shook the hand of each one before reclaiming her original spot. She was nervous and fidgeted, sliding her hands in and out of her pockets. Clearing her throat. Moving back and forth on her heels.

Choice, who as her friend knew her trepidation so well, gave her an encouraging smile.

"Unlike myself, all of you are so experienced in your fields and I am grateful to have you here to assist me in ensuring so many children aged out of the foster care system receive the help they deserve and need," she said, hearing the slight tremble in her voice.

The women all offered her smiles.

Monica didn't reveal that she'd taken both a business and a website-development course at Manhattan Community College as a nondegree student. She hoped that, plus her two years of college, would give her better footing alongside these very competent women.

"I'm so nervous," she admitted with a laugh. "Please forgive me."

"You're doing fine, darlin'," Kylie said, holding steadfast to her Charleston accent although she'd moved to the northeast over twenty years ago.

"How about the space? Does everyone like it?" Monica asked as she looked about the office at the khaki decor with accents in coral, turquoise, citrine and gold.

"It's beautiful," everyone agreed.

She crossed the room, loving how the fall sun gleamed through the windows and lit the tiled floor as she reached the small office she'd reserved for herself. Here, the same hues from the outer office continued with a large bouquet of fresh flowers on the edge of her clear desk. She moved to push the rolling ergonomic chair out of the office, setting it at the head of the wide aisle running up the middle of the desks. "So, let's update each other before Montgomery and Choice have to go," she said, turning to close the door behind her before sitting down and crossing her legs.

The women all moved to their assigned desks, as well.

"We already have a list of ten applicants sent over from different county social service departments," Kylie began. "I've placed them on your desk."

Monica was personally funding awards of five thousand dollars each from money she'd gifted the foundation. "Reach out to other agencies in the tristate area. There are more people who need help. Let's find them," she said.

"Right away, boss," Kylie said.

Boss? I'm a boss! I like it.

She turned to Nylah.

The woman opened up a coral folder on her desk. "I think our plan should be to reach out to large companies who offer local community grants. I researched and I can meet the current deadlines of ten such corporations. I just need to adjust the grant I've already written to meet specific guidelines."

"I didn't even know these brands offered grant money like that," Monica admitted after accepting the folder and looking at the names listed.

"That's my job," Nylah said. "And I believe in what you're doing. Remember, I aged out of the foster care system myself."

Monica gave her a heartfelt smile. "Thank you," she said with feeling before turning to Choice.

"The majority of my work was done in the setting up of the foundation," she said. "I won't be here in the office, but The Bridge Foundation is a client and Monica knows how to reach out to me if a legal matter arises."

The women all nodded in understanding.

"And Montgomery," Monica said, turning to the braided beauty who looked divine in a fuchsia pantsuit with turquoise heels.

"Like Choice, I will be working from my own offices, but I agreed with Monica that we all should meet on this first day and put faces to the names," Montgomery said, giving each woman a winning smile before focusing her sharp gaze back on Monica. "We have gotten a lot of traction from the press kits that were sent out, but even more requests for an interview with you have come in."

"No," Monica said with a shake of her head.

The publicist had made it clear she wanted the still-reserved Monica to become the face of the organization. Tell her story. Try to connect with the same people she was trying to help. Try to pull at the heartstrings—and wallets—of wealthy donors.

And use my connection to my father to help promote it all.

Something the NDA would not allow. She shared a brief look with Choice, who was aware of the agreement as her attorney.

"Maybe not live interviews," Choice suggested. "But taped interviews with specific guidelines and editorial control might work best."

Monica looked pensive.

"Or speaking engagements minus Q & As," Montgomery suggested. "Especially as we gear up for the charity gala in a few months."

Monica released a breath as she turned a bit in her chair to look out the window. Sunlight broke through the towering buildings, and the skies were a beautiful blue backdrop for the concrete-and-steel structures. In that moment of quiet she was facing—and trying to conquer—her fear...

Of public speaking,

Of more public scrutiny.

Of more reminders that her father gave her away.

She tried and failed. "No," she said, forcing finality into her tone as she felt waves of relief at not stepping out of the shadows. "My intention was never to be the face or the brand or whatever marketing term it is. I just want to help foster kids, not become some pseudo celebrity. Remember for the last five years, I worked as a maid and lived seen yet not seen—if that makes any sense."

"It does," Choice said, offering her a warm and encouraging smile.

"Give me some time to adjust to everything and we'll see. Okay?" she said.

Montgomery nodded. "You're the boss," she said.

I'm the boss.

Monica glanced out the window again and smiled at the very idea of that. As they ended the meeting and Choice and Montgomery took their leave, she retrieved her briefcase from the seating area and made her way with her chair to her office, closing the door behind her. She set her things atop the desk and moved over to the lone window in the corner, crossing her arms over her chest as she looked out at the world where she was trying to carve her own little place.

Am I crazy? Can I do this?

She shifted her sight to focus on her reflection in the glass. *The only way to do it is to do it.*

Bzzzzzz.

Monica jumped, surprised by the sudden noise. She

whirled to see the electric-blue light of the intercom system flashing.

Calm down, Mo.

She stepped over to the desk to press the button as she cleared her throat. "Yes?"

"Mr. Cress to see you."

Monica felt warmth as her grin spread. "Send him in. Thank you," she added, holding up her hands and grimacing before pressing the button again.

Quickly she struck several poses. Leaning against the corner of her desk. By the window. In the seat behind her desk. Finally, in the second before the door opened, she came from behind the desk and simply walked over to meet him.

"Hello, beautiful," he said, closing the door and pressing a kiss to her jawline as she slipped her arms around his waist.

She inhaled deeply of his scent and released a low moan. "You always smell so good," she sighed, allowing herself a kiss to his neck before stepping away with reluctance. "I thought we were meeting up for an early dinner?"

He gave her that look. The charming one. The one that easily beguiled. The setup before the letdown. And there had been plenty lately.

She tensed. Missed dates and rescheduling plans were becoming commonplace as he became more focused on opening his own restaurant. Securing investors. Scouting locations.

At least I hope that's all it is.

Over the last few weeks, they'd seen each other just

a few times. Phone calls and FaceTime had replaced real contact. She felt the void.

"I have to cancel dinner," he admitted.

"Again," she said, forcing a smile as she glanced over at him while she took her seat behind her desk.

The energy in the room shifted. It was hard to miss. Lately it had become familiar.

"Monica."

She looked up at him.

"There was a time you encouraged me to chase my dream," he said, his tone a little hard.

"You think I *discourage* you now?" she asked. "Really, Gabe?"

He looked up at the ceiling briefly before walking over to stand beside her. He turned her chair to face him as he squatted before her and cupped her knees with his hands. "I came to tell you I am proud of you. The foundation. Your confidence. Your need to help," he said, his eyes searching hers.

Monica bit her bottom lip to keep her emotions from overtaking her. She believed every word he spoke and the look of pride in his eyes.

"The restaurant is going to take up more of my time," he admitted, reaching up to stroke her jawline with his thumb, which drew a shiver. "But I'm not going anywhere. I'm here. With you. In this. So into this. Us."

Her breaths filled the silence.

"For the first time, I want it all. The success, proving my family wrong and standing up for myself," he implored.

She turned her head to press a kiss to his hand.

"Okay?" he asked.

The breath she released was shaky. Of late she had begun to worry that Gabe had wanted their relationship once she had risen above the station of maid and they'd end once he realized that not even her sudden wealth would make her good enough for him.

What if I'd never received the inheritance? Would he have given me a second look at all?

She nodded. "Okay," she said, feeling foolish for doubting him.

Gabe felt six pairs of eyes bore into him. The den where they were seated was quiet. He didn't try to fill it. He'd said what he needed to say. Now he waited. He looked over at his father as he swirled the ice in his snifter of scotch.

Phillip Sr. stared out of the window as he stroked the hairs of his chin and silently clenched and unclenched his jaw.

"One less dog in the race for CEO then," Cole said, raising his bottle of beer in a toast and inclining his head.

Gabe looked down into the amber liquid in his crystal glass. The sound of glass crashing against the wall echoed violently. He looked up just as his father lowered his swinging arm and stared at him. The move was pure intimidation.

Gabe felt offended by it. Ridiculed. He notched his chin higher and met his father's glare with one of his own.

I'm not backing down. Not caving. Not putting your

*needs before mine. Not to make you proud and then
fail, because there is no way to please you.*

After long tense moments where it felt everyone
in the room held their breath, Phillip Sr. stormed out.
Gabe took a deep sip of his drink as he turned from
the stunned look in his mother's blue eyes.

"No man—or woman—should divide a family,"
she said.

Monica.

"No woman did," he said, his voice hardened in
defense of her. "It's funny that Monica was someone
we all trusted in our home and in our lives for the last
five years, but now that she is involved with me—"

Nicolette scoffed audibly. "Trust. More like tolerated out of necessity," she said in French.

"Penser plus haut, mère." He admonished her in
French to think higher.

Her face flushed in anger as she eyed him. He was
used to seeing her gaze filled with adoration, not brimming with annoyance. *"Prends tes propres conseils,
fiston,"* she said, her voice soft.

Gabe swallowed her words of taking his own advice
down with his drink. He turned his back on her and
the revelation of her classist beliefs. He'd never realized they ran so deep. That was deeply disappointing.

"Family should be together," she said from behind
him in French.

"And not at war," he countered, giving voice to his
frustration with his father's controlling hand in his life.

Silence.

He turned, ignoring his brothers, to look at her.

"Your father has his reasons" was all that she said.

"And he also has sons who are grown men and deserve his respect," he said, unable to keep the edge from his tone. "Not be treated as pawns on a chessboard."

Nicolette rose and smoothed her hands over the turquoise-and-silver silk caftan she wore. She moved about the room and stroked the cheek of each of her sons.

"Nous vous adorons tous. Plus qu'on ne le sait. Plus que ce qu'on montre. S'il te plaît, n'oublie jamais ça. S'il vous plaît," she said, coming to Gabriel and patting under his chin.

"We adore you all. More than we know. More than we show. Please never forget that. Please."

And like always, his mother took her leave to be by his father's side—be he right or wrong. One thing he couldn't deny was their loyalty to each other. Even when it pitted her against her sons.

"You're a fool," Phillip Jr. said with a shake of his head as he rose to his feet and buttoned the jacket of his custom-made suit before striding to the door. "Did you really believe he would finance a solo restaurant after you stepped down from Cress, INC.?"

"And you're a bigger fool if you think I haven't already secured investors," Gabe said, his voice hard and unrelenting. "I just hoped my family would support me in this. Same way I would support any of you in following your dreams...*bro.*"

One by one his brothers took their leave, most likely to seek out their parents and ensure they understood they were not in agreement with their brother. All except Cole.

"Aren't you going to kiss the ring, too?" Gabe asked, never before feeling so divided from his own family and never more determined to make his solo restaurant a success.

"There's a better chance of me kissing his butt and you know it," Cole drawled, rising from the low-slung sofa.

Gabe noticed a slow half smile on his brother's face and followed his line of vision across the wide space to land on Chef Jillian leaving the pantry to enter the kitchen.

"Now that's a behind I love kissing," Cole said.

Gabe's eyebrows rose in surprise. "*Chef* Jillian?" he asked.

Cole stopped in his tracks with his face incredulous. "Monica *the Maid*?" he shot back.

Gabe smiled. "Checkmate," he said.

He was with the maid and his brother had an ongoing dalliance with the chef. Their mother would have a conniption. Their father's head might literally explode.

"How is that going?" his brother asked, standing in the open doorway with his hands pushed deep into the pockets of his denims.

Gabe thought of Monica. The way her emotions were mirrored in her doe-shaped eyes. Be it happiness, anger, annoyance or passion. And her scent. He could close his eyes and find her in the crowd just using his nose. Or her intelligence, which he admitted surprised him when she offered such insight and unique perspective on things he took for granted. And the sex. Best ever. Period. Never had he felt so out of control in bed. And he liked it.

"Going good" was all that he confessed.

Cole nodded.

"And the chef?" Gabe asked.

Cole shrugged one broad shoulder. "It is what it is and ain't what it ain't," he said, pulling his iPhone from his back pocket.

"Careful, little brother, sometimes what you think it *ain't*, it actually becomes, and before you know it, you're in the thick of it, needing someone you didn't even know you would want," Gabe said, revealing a little more of just what Monica had come to mean to him.

He looked from Cole to the chef as his brother tapped away on the phone before lowering it to look over at Jillian. Gabe followed his line of vision, his curiosity piqued.

Jillian reached for her own cell phone. Across the divide she looked up. She and Cole shared a brief but very telling look before she typed away as she turned and walked back into the pantry, leaving the door ajar.

Ding.

Cole read the text that was clearly from Jillian in response to his, and he smiled so hard his dimples showed. "To be honest, I might just be ready for a little more than I expected, big brother," he said before crossing the den and then the kitchen. He looked around for any other witnesses besides Gabe before joining their pretty chef in the pantry.

Gabe didn't dare to think about what was going on beyond the closed door. Not at all.

"Nah," he said aloud as he crossed the den, and the kitchen, as well, to reach the elevator for a ride up to the fourth floor.

As soon as it stopped and he opened the gate, he walked over to the glass wall that ran up the entire rear of the house. Crossing his arms over his chest and spreading his legs wide, he looked out at the snow-covered backyard. The whiteness was stark and pure, particularly against the night.

Almost as pure as his intentions when he'd humbled himself and asked for his father's help in launching his own eatery. The decision to leave Cress, INC. had not been easy. Asking his father to financially back him had been even harder. Having the majority of his family aligned against him had been the worst. Still holding his drink, he turned from the view and looked around at the den, taking in the black-and-white family photos on the custom shelves and high-end tables. Memories made over the last forty years or better. Bonds being slowly shattered before his eyes over greed, forced competition and loyalty that was blind to anything but his father's wishes.

Anger and annoyance caused his grip on his glass to tighten. If he was honest with himself, there was pain and regret in the mix of his feelings. He felt foolish for even a sliver of hope that his family would support him.

Gabe pulled out his iPhone and called Monica. It rang twice. "Hey, you," he said. "You busy?"

"I can get unbusy with the right motivation," she said.

He smiled. "I'm sending a car to bring you to where I will be waiting for you," he said.

"And where is that?" she asked, her voice husky soft.

Gabe entered his bedroom suite and quickly packed an overnight bag. "It's a surprise," he said.

"Panties or no panties?" she teased.

He paused. His heart thundered. "No panties is *always* the default answer."

"Fun."

They ended the call.

He slung his bag over his shoulder and left his room to make his way back to the elevator. He rode it down to the basement, smirking a bit at how quickly he'd reverted back to his teenage days of sneaking out of the town house and avoiding his family by using the servants' entrance in the basement. He just wasn't in the mood for more confrontation. It was pointless.

Besides, he was on a mission that needed no interruptions.

Gabe stepped out and paused, looking down the hall to the quarters where Monica had once lived. Over the years, he had ventured to the cellar only to retrieve wine, and never once thought of her. For him, she'd been invisible. Someone to clean and help keep his living space orderly. Before they'd become intimate, he'd given no thought to her life outside of her part in theirs.

"More like tolerated out of necessity."

As he remembered his mother's words, he worried that maybe he was not very different from his parents.

Disturbed by that thought, he turned and made his way down the left side of the hall and past the glass door of the laundry room to the exit. He made sure the exit was securely closed before taking the steps two at a time until he reached the street. The car service he'd requested awaited him, and Gabe took a deep, invigorating breath of the winter winds as he allowed himself a look up at the town house before climbing into the rear of the SUV.

The ride was brief. Less than twenty minutes. For that, he was glad.

He spotted Monica leaving her own vehicle double-parked in front of the building. The winds whipped her hair and ruffled the ball-shaped fur she wore with jeans and thigh-high boots. She turned and smiled as he exited his vehicle with his bag in hand and stepped onto the sidewalk to pull her body close to his for a kiss. She deepened it, surprising him. As they got lost in one another, the noise and congestion of the city faded. The frigid cold and icy snow seemed to melt away. The fast-moving bodies breezing past them on the street were gone.

"Let's go up," Gabe said, breaking their connection with reluctance as he reached for her hand and led her inside the towering building.

"Up to where, exactly?" Monica asked, brushing her hair back from her face as she looked around at the modern design of the lobby.

The uniformed concierge gave them a welcoming smile and nod.

"My apartment," he finally said as they reached the set of four elevators.

She paused.

He looked at her as he pushed the button. Her expression was guarded. "What's wrong?" he asked as she took the final step to be back at his side.

As the doors slid open and they stepped onto the lift, she forced a smile, but it didn't reach her eyes. He reached for her hand and stroked her palm with his thumb as he used his free hand to press the button for the twenty-fourth floor. "What's wrong, Monica?" he repeated.

She shook her head and released his hand to wrap her arms around his waist. "Not a thing, *Gabriel*," she said, saying his name teasingly as she raised her face to press a kiss to his chin. "Congratulations on your new apartment."

He smiled, but he felt his own unease.

After the elevator came to a smooth stop and as they made their way to the apartment, he eyed her. He had come to know Monica well, and when something worried her, she became distant and quiet. Getting her to open up about it seemed to make her withdraw even more.

"This is nice, Gabe," she said, removing her coat as she moved about the furnished, two-thousand-square-foot space in the Midtown Park Avenue South building. "I didn't know you were even looking to move out from your parents'."

He eyed her as he dropped his bag on the sectional sofa, removed his overcoat and kicked off his shoes. "It was time."

Which was on her mind? That I moved or that I didn't tell her?

Monica looked over her shoulder at him as he joined her at the floor-to-ceiling windows, which were offering a spectacular view of the city landscape at night. "Are things worse with your family?" she asked.

"They'll come around," he said, dipping his head to press a kiss to her throat before he moved over to the electric fireplace to light it.

"I hope so," she said, crossing the wide-plank wood floors to stand beside him before the fire. "The last thing I want for you is to ever know what it feels like to not have family, Gabe."

He thought of the childhood she rarely spoke of and felt regret that her upbringing had been bleak at times. She wrapped her arms around him, and he looked down at her as she looked up at him. Her eyes were soft, and the flames of the fire flicked in their depths. She gave him the hint of a smile as she eased her hands under his sweater and massaged his lower back, evoking goose bumps across his skin.

Gabe felt breathless, and something profound and deep clutched at his chest as he let his eyes take in every aspect of her face. Missing nothing. Captivated by it all.

Their kisses began as light touches of their lips as they stared at one another almost playfully. They tasted of one another with deep, guttural moans of pleasure. Slowly they undressed each other, illuminated by the fire's light as night darkened their surroundings.

Gabe lifted her body up and she wrapped her arms and legs around him as he hotly licked at her mouth. The feel of her softness against him and the scent of her—that heady mix of sweet perfume and woman—lengthened his inches with hardness that rose up against her buttocks.

Monica leaned back enough to look down at him. She kissed him. Softly. With a tempting smile that he knew he would never forget, she stroked the back of his head before guiding his mouth to her breasts. With a grunt, he latched on and deeply sucked her nipple as he pressed his face into the softness and gripped her hips to guide her downward. The first feel of her heat and wetness against his tip caused him to hiss, in that hot little moment before she arched her hips to take all of him inside her.

They gasped and clung to one another.

He fought for control, not wanting his pleasure at the very feel of her intimacy gripping him to push him to a speedy end. And when she began to slowly circle her hips, sending her core up and down the length of him, he bent one leg and reached out to press one hand against the wall—looking for help to keep them from losing balance as he felt lost in a haze of passion and desire.

No words were spoken. Just panted breaths and deep gasps echoed as sweat coated their bodies from the heat of lovemaking and the fireplace. He was lost. Gone. She used her muscles to grip and release his tool as she rode him. With his free hand, he gripped her buttock as he licked and sucked at her breasts, loving each tremble and purr of pleasure he drew from her. He felt her climax nearing and took control, turning to drop them down onto the sofa, then arched his back and drove his hardness inside with swiftness and depth until soon they both cried out with a roughness that only hinted at the wildness they felt as they climaxed together.

And long after their cries subsided, their pulses slowed and the sweet addictive haze of climaxing died down, she lay atop him on the couch. His knees were bent and open as he listened to her long breaths as she slept. He turned his head to cast his gaze on the fire as he thought of that moment earlier when he had felt something profound for Monica. The captivation. The warmth spreading across his chest. Breathlessness.

He closed his eyes and clenched his jaw as he pushed away the memory and everything it could mean. A hint of feelings he was not ready to accept.

Ten

Three months later

Was it possible to truly feel like Cinderella?

Monica did.

As she looked at her reflection in the glass, she didn't notice the panoramic view of the New York skyline and Hudson River on the other side of it or the well-dressed people enjoying the colorful, carnival-themed gala behind her. The strapless white silk couture gown she wore seemed to gleam, and the Swarovski crystals sewn into a modern design across the bodice twinkled like stardust. A tight corseted waist and attached skirt gave her a buxom shape, while the thigh-high slit sexily exposed her leg. Her hair was piled atop her head, elongating her neck and showcasing her bared shoulders.

She smiled, remembering the days when she imagined the life she was now living. When she could get close to gowns like the one she wore only if she allowed herself a few minutes of folly in the closets of Nicolette and Raquel. Sometimes she felt she was in a fairy tale and someone would close the book and bring it all to an end, with her leaving a glass shoe on the stairs.

"Congratulations, Monica."

She stiffened, instantly recognizing the voice of Nicolette Cress. She gave herself one last look before turning to face Gabe's mother. The woman looked beautiful in a dark blue chiffon maxi dress with a plunging neckline. "Thank you... Nicolette," she said, never having addressed her by her first name before.

The act brought a small smile to the woman's face.

"I wasn't aware that you purchased a ticket," Monica continued, proud that she'd shown no trepidation or even the curiosity she felt at seeing Nicolette at her event.

"You captured the attention of a few of my friends who are in attendance and I thought it might be my only chance to see my son," Nicolette said, taking a sip from the flute of champagne she held as she came to stand beside her at the window.

Monica's gut clenched. "He's running late. There was a problem with the restaurant, and there's an important inspection first thing in the morning," she explained, giving her the same excuse Gabe had given her just a little over an hour ago.

Nicolette gave her a tight smile. "Never had I imagined the day I would need updates on my son from his bedmate," she said with a release of a heavy breath.

Monica's grip on her ball-shaped clutch tightened. "Bedmate?" she asked. "It seems you need an update on that, as well."

Some emotion filled the woman's blue eyes.

Monica couldn't quite place it.

"I only want what's best for Gabriel—for all of my sons," she said, her French accent heavy.

Monica used to find it fascinating. "And I'm not it?" she asked.

"Long-term?" Nicolette asked. "No."

Monica tensed, hating how the woman gave voice to her concern with such ease. Over the last few months, her relationship with Gabe had become strained as his sole focus was preparing for the opening of his restaurant. He seemed to be constantly canceling dates or showing up late, and when they were together his mind was clearly elsewhere. She told herself he was just focused on his success and things would go back to the norm, but she couldn't fight off the nagging belief the sexy playboy had tired of the relationship and would leave her behind.

In truth she had already begun to withdraw, limit her expectations and steel herself for a breakup, but she doubted he even noticed.

"Shouldn't this be a conversation you have with Gabe?" Monica asked.

"Why? When it's clear *you're* the cause for the division?"

Monica frowned, unable not to do so. "You're wrong,

Nicolette, because the very last thing I want is for Gabe to be divided from his family," she said, her conviction clear in her voice.

"Yet I didn't see my son for Thanksgiving, Christmas nor New Year's Day."

"True, Gabe and I spent those holidays together, but I encouraged him to spend them with his family," she said, in truth. "Especially after the childhood I had."

Nicolette tapped the tips of her nude nails against her flute as she walked behind Monica to reach her other side. "It is your upbringing that is exactly why this *thing* you two have going will not work. Money cannot erase the indelible mark it left on your life."

"You know nothing of my life. You never cared to," Monica said, feeling offended and judged.

Nicolette arched a brow. "You were my maid, not my friend," she countered.

"And that was sufficient for me, as well, but never claim to know me. That would be a big mistake, *Nicolette*," she said with coldness.

The woman smiled, but it did not replace the anger in her eyes. "You lived and worked in my home for five years, so don't convince yourself I hate you."

"And please don't convince yourself that I was envious of you," Monica countered. "Because if it was my intention to come between Gabe and your family, then I would have revealed to him that he and his brother were under surveillance at the direction of you, your husband or both."

Nicolette looked surprised at Monica knowing that.

Monica looked down at the floor and smiled as she

copied the woman's move and walked behind her to stand on her other side. "Tonight is not the night for this. After those five years working and living in your home, I know you are a woman who holds dear decorum and appropriate behavior," she said. "Tonight is huge for me and my foundation. A celebration. Not an opportunity to belittle me to my face, to judge my relationship with your son or to manipulate me into doing something that suits you. So out of respect for Gabe, as his mother, I am asking you to leave and let me enjoy the night. You're welcome to stay and appreciate the festivities, but please leave if your goal is to make me feel beneath you."

Nicolette stopped a passing waiter and set her near-empty flute on the tray. "I'll leave," she said. "You're right. I was out of line. Accept my apology for that. But still heed my warning. Anything serious between you and Gabe will not work or last."

"Have a good night, Nicolette," Monica said.

"I can see in your eyes that you know I'm right."

Monica said nothing, hating that the woman spoke to her very insecurities about her relationship with Gabe. "Good night," she repeated, her tone firm.

In the glass, she watched the reflection of the woman finally turn and retreat.

Monica closed her eyes and shook her head a little as she pinched the bridge of her nose. The urge to pull her phone from her clutch and call Gabe came, but she pushed the idea away. The disappointment of him missing most of the night stung. Truly, she didn't even want to hear his voice. Not even enough to tell him his mother had just ambushed her.

Now she really felt like Cinderella, complete with a wicked stepmother.

Just no Prince Charming.

"Ready?"

She opened her eyes at the sound of Montgomery's voice. In the glass, she shifted her gaze to the reflection of the four women standing behind her. Choice, Montgomery, Kylie and Nylah. Her team. Each had worked so hard to make the night a success. She was grateful for each one. Professional alliances had become friendships.

And even that was a sign of her healing from her past. She'd never seen the need to make friends when she'd never known when her time at that particular group home or foster family would end.

With a deep breath, she turned to face them, knowing the time had come. She had walked the red carpet. Effortlessly avoided questions about her father and about her relationship with Gabe. Pretended not to be starstruck by the long list of A-list actors and singers, celebrities, and social media influencers Montgomery and her team had convinced to attend. Greeted her guests at the carnival-style event that she'd completely co-opted from the Cress Family Foundation gala she'd attended. Made the rounds. Taken photos with the fifty foster care children who had been awarded funds to help them transition to adulthood.

And now the biggest test was next.

"Yes," she said, feeling nervous. "It's now or never."

Together the ladies walked through the crowd of the Fifth Avenue venue with its 360-degree view of the metropolis at night. After Montgomery motioned for the live band to slow and lower its upbeat music, Monica took the microphone she handed her. She looked on at the colorful lighting, abundant floral arrangements and room filled with elegantly dressed people, there to support her vision. She pressed her free hand against her belly hoping to settle the butterflies.

"Good evening, everyone," she said. "Just a quick break in the evening to thank you all for attending tonight's event and for the money we raised from your generous donations that will allow us to fund our very important effort to financially support young adults who, like myself, were aged out of the foster care system and left to figure it out on their own—a scary effort, I promise you."

She paused, hating how in that moment she would love to look out at the edge of the crowd and see Gabe standing there. Watching her. Willing her to fight her fear and press on. Quickly her eyes scanned the parts of the crowd she could see. She was disappointed but unsurprised to not see him. It stung.

"To date we have been able to assist more than one hundred such fearless people with their dreams to grow beyond their circumstances. I cannot thank you all enough for your support. I am moved beyond words and honored beyond measure…whatever the reason," she added, knowing that many of the celebrities were in attendance out of allegiance to her father and pity at her story.

Servers filed into the room, carrying trays of crystal flutes filled with champagne. Monica accepted one. "I just want to thank my entire team for their support and all of you for ensuring a successful launch of this nonprofit foundation," she said, raising her glass high in the air. "Here's to The Bridge."

"The Bridge," everyone said in unison.

She smiled, turning to touch her glass to those Choice, Montgomery, Kylie and Nylah held, before finally taking a deep sip as the room filled with applause. With one final smile, Monica handed over the microphone as Montgomery motioned for the band to resume their playing. Fraught with nerves and unsure if she'd said the right things, and wondering what these strangers whispered about her, she made her way across the room and onto the elevator to reach the roof.

The chill immediately surrounded her, and she shivered as she released a stream of breath that was visible in the frosty air. She allowed herself a moment to pretend the cold was nothing as she thought of her life just a year ago and how everything—*everything*—had changed.

"Thank you," she whispered up to the heavens.

She looked out at the city. The lights amid the darkness. The pockets of warmth in the cold. The snow blanketing the streets and the tops of the sky-high buildings. The familiar noise. She loved Manhattan. It helped to heal her. Gave her a place to finally call home.

She would love nothing more than to share this moment with—

"Monica."

Gabe.

Her heart pounded just as it did every time she saw him. She turned just as he rushed across the snow-covered roof, removing his overcoat to place it around her bared shoulders. "It's freezing up here," he said as he pulled her body into his embrace.

She welcomed his warmth but resented yet another late appearance.

"At least he showed up this time."

Gabe stiffened and leaned back from her. His eyes searched her face as he frowned a little.

"What?" she asked in confusion.

"At least I showed up this time?" he asked.

Her mouth fell open. She realized she had said the words aloud and not in her head. "Yes," she said, accepting that they were her truth and they deserved to finally be given voice.

His frown deepened as he slid his hands into the pockets of his tuxedo pants.

She stepped back from him, trying so hard not to notice how devastatingly handsome he looked in his black tuxedo. *So damn good.*

"I called and explained what happened," Gabe said before glancing up as snow began to lightly fall.

Monica did the same. "Yes, you did. You always call with an explanation…of why you're late, why you're canceling, why you're not even making plans to see me anymore," she said, as she held up a hand to let one single snowflake float down upon it. "Making phone calls is not the problem."

"What is?" he asked.

She crushed the snowflake inside her fist. "I can only guess," she said, looking anywhere but at him. "I don't know why you're fading out of this relationship, but you are. First your family and now me, I guess."

"My family?"

"Yes!" she stressed and then took a breath to reclaim her calm. "If you can cut them off and move out and be okay with not having them in your life, what does that say about your loyalty to me?"

"So now I'm disloyal?" Gabe asked, his voice low.

"And I'm divisive?" she countered.

"What?" he asked, obviously confused.

Monica knew she was all over the place. So were her emotions. Even in the storm of her anger, she knew she could find temporary calm in his arms. It would be so easy to push aside her fears and her annoyance to just get lost in him. Holding him. Kissing him.

"Deny that your family blames me for the distance between you," she said.

His eyes shifted. That was telling.

So, Nicolette had voiced her issues with me to him already.

"You have nothing to do with the way things are between me and some of my family," he said, not directly answering her question.

Gabe was not a liar.

"But I don't want you to take them for granted because you don't know what it feels like to not have family," she said, wishing the feeling wasn't so familiar to her.

"I don't want to be taken for granted either, Monica," he countered.

"Yes, but if you can walk away from them so easily—"

Gabe frowned. "You think my decision to stand independently was easy?"

She shrugged. "It seems to be."

He snorted in derision. "A lot of things aren't what they seem," he said, giving her a once-over before looking away from her.

She stiffened. "If you meant that for me, you're wrong, because I am exactly what I claim to be."

"Supportive? Understanding? Selfless?" he asked, his voice filled with censure. "You're the one in the wrong."

Monica gathered her skirt in her hands as she marched over to stand before him. "Not supportive? Not understanding? Anything but selfless? Me?" she asked, poking his chest with her index finger after each question. "Are you crazy?"

"Are you?" he shot back.

"To think you would ever see me as your equal after I was your maid?" she asked. "Yes, I just might be."

Gabe's face hardened. "I left behind the workers at my restaurant to try and share some of the night with you," he said, his tone as stiff as his face. "And you greet me with complaints."

"Not complaints. Just truth," she said, lowering her hands and balling them into tight fists that pressed the tips of her nails into the flesh of her palm.

"I don't need this shit right now, Monica! Not from

you," he said, his voice rising and battling with the sounds of the metropolis, which filled the chilly night air.

"When?" she said quietly.

Gabe paused with his chest heaving. "What?" he asked, his face a mask of confusion.

"Over the last few months, you've barely given me the time of day, so when should we have talked?" she asked, remembering nights where she'd sat fully dressed and disappointed because a mishap at the site of the restaurant kept him from showing up for a date.

Gabe eyed her with intensity as he smoothed his hand over the shadow of his beard before turning to walk away from her, then suddenly turned again. "I thought you understood how important this restaurant was for me. If I mistook that, I apologize, but I won't pretend that it doesn't need or deserve my attention right now, Monica," he said.

"And I don't?" Monica asked.

Their eyes locked.

The distance between them seemed more like miles than just a few feet.

"Am I fighting a losing battle, Monica?" he asked.

She eyed him for as long as she could without feeling the urge to run to him. "Meaning?"

"My time is important, too. Am I wasting mine with you?" he asked, pausing as he raised one hand and began to tick off each finger. "I hate my family. I'm never around. I'm fading like the invisible man. I'm disloyal. What else? Let 'em roll."

Would you still be with me if I was still a maid?

She set aside her thought as some emotion flashed

in his eyes. For the briefest moment she thought it was pain but decided she was wrong. Just like she had been wrong about so many things.

Like thinking this could work.

She thought of his mother—her words, her desire for them to end. Between Monica's insecurities and his ambition would Nicolette Cress whispering her objections to her son be the nail in the coffin of their relationship? She knew firsthand the Cresses were a tight-knit bunch.

She fell silent. The fracture between Gabe and his family was deepening. She felt she'd played a major role in that. She knew all too well what it felt like to be without family. That was something she wished on no one.

"If you think so lowly of me, why be with me?" he asked.

"And if I'm not making you happy, why not tell me?" she shot back.

Gabe shook his head as he clenched his jaw. "Is it possible to make you happy?" he asked.

She felt chilled to the bone by the coldness of his tone. The weather around them was warm in comparison.

"Don't be a jerk, Gabe," she said.

He scowled. "My apologies. I'll just add it to your list of complaints," he muttered as he began to pace.

"Screw you!" she snapped.

He splayed his hands. "And take the chance of you complaining about it? Hell no!" he shot back.

"You are an ass!"

He raised his hand and emphatically ticked off another finger.

She glared at him.

Gabe opened his mouth but shut it again as he rolled his shoulders, as if seeking to be tension-free. He took a large inhale and then exhaled. "What do you want from me?" he asked.

All of you.

The thought came with a swiftness and scared her. She was hesitant to reveal just how necessary Gabriel Cress had become to her. Not when she wasn't sure his desire of her was equal. "To not feel like a second thought," she said, confessing to that.

Gabe looked around at the snow falling around them. "The very last thing you are to me, Monica Darby, is a second thought," he admitted.

Her heart soared.

"But—" he stopped.

She arched a brow and tilted her head to the side as she eyed him brushing snowflakes from his shoulders. "But," she repeated to fill his pause.

"I don't know if you will ever believe that," he said, looking back at her. "And I don't know how to prove it to you. Not if it means ignoring my dreams. I want this restaurant—I need this restaurant—to succeed and that means hard work and focus."

"So if I asked you to roll it all back? Stop being so dogged in your pursuit of success, mend the divide between you and your family, find a balance between what you want and what you need…?" she said, walking over to sandwich one of his hands between both of hers.

"And if I asked you if you would ever be able to fully trust me?" he returned.

Neither answered the question they were asked.

"So you choose that restaurant over everything and everyone," she said, holding up the collars of his coat to turn her face and bury her nose against the lightweight black wool. His scent—the one she loved—clung to it.

"And you choose to hold anything and everything against me."

Am I?

Then she remembered how she'd felt all night without him there and how the lack of his presence had become commonplace. How she had begun to envision her life without him. Preparing herself for that moment when it ended and even contemplating ending it herself to avoid feeling so helpless.

To leave and not be left...

"Why did we think this would work?" she asked, her voice low.

"If you think it's not damn working, then why are we wasting our time!" he roared, splaying his hands angrily. "To hell with it if that's how you feel."

Her ire matched his. "Then to hell with it, Gabe," she shouted back.

"This is ridiculous!"

"Thinking you don't need anyone is ridiculous!"

"I damn sure don't need *this* right now."

She looked over at him as her eyes widened. "Don't let me force you to be here," she said.

He squinted as he eyed her for a long moment that seemed to tick by slowly before he turned and walked over to the elevator.

"Gabe," she called to him as her heart galloped full speed in its race to its break.

I can see in your eyes that you know I'm right.

Nicolette's words seemed to echo inside her. Mocking her.

You know I'm right.

You know I'm right.

You know I'm right.

She blinked and shook her head to free it of the woman's voice. She removed his coat and crossed the short distance to press it against his chest before releasing it without a care if he caught it or let it slip and fall. She felt his hand reach for hers and she pulled away from his touch turning her back on him. "It started on a roof with you in a tux and looks like it's ending the same way," she said with a bitter little laugh.

At his continued silence, she looked back over her shoulder to find she was alone.

Hours later Gabe sat in his apartment looking at the Manhattan skyline as he nursed his snifter of his favorite scotch as the heat of the lit fireplace warmed him. His thoughts were full and troubled.

When he arrived at her event and then rushed to the roof to find her, never had he guessed the night would end with them going their separate ways. He'd fought hard not to feel ambushed as she'd revealed to him all the misgivings she'd obviously had about him all along. His stomach clenched and his grip on the glass tightened.

He wasn't quite sure what emotions he felt swirling inside him, but anger was one. Indignation was another. For many reasons. For her lack of trust. Her belief in the very worst about him. And her willingness to end it when all he wanted was more time to make his restaurant a success—something he revealed to her early on.

Or at least he thought he had.

He released a heavy breath and took another sip.

He knew of her past, and that loyalty and trust might be issues for her—for them—but he'd never doubted that Monica would doubt him. Not see him. Not know him. Not understand him. That bothered him. He knew he had lost his focus and had become so driven that it seemed nothing else mattered but the restaurant. He'd thought she understood just how important this was to him, particularly knowing that his family had offered him no help nor support and, to him, held a desire for him to fail just so they could say, "I told you so."

He'd wanted to do anything but fail and had expressed that to her.

He'd never been one to take on a losing battle and let it defeat him.

He'd made a choice between his relationship and ambition before. Time and time again, his ambition had won. It hadn't been a conscious choice to make her feel unwanted and undesired. His desire to have her in his life had never been in question for him.

But in that moment when he'd reached for her hand

and felt compelled to fight for her—to fight for them—she'd snatched hers away. He let it be. He let her be. He let her go.

Because he knew how important his success was to him. He knew there had been a choice to be made, and without her support and belief in him as an honorable, hardworking man who was driven, he had felt there had been no other choice than to tuck his head, focus on his work and get the job done. For him, he'd chosen something he could believe in. Her fears had him concerned she would never trust in him enough to not judge everything he did.

But as the hours ticked by and the truth settled in, he wasn't as sure of his choice.

Still, it had not been his alone.

She had seemed to accept that it was done and was prepared to move on.

It wasn't what he wanted. He missed her already, but he was accepting that perhaps their breakup was for the best.

He looked up at the framed photo of himself and Monica that sat on the mantel of the fireplace. They'd been skiing in Aspen, and Monica, who had felt completely out of her element, had fallen off her skis and he'd purposely tumbled down beside her and pulled out his phone to capture their laughter in a selfie.

They'd played in the snow all day and created their own heat together all night.

"Damn," he swore, setting his glass on the metal end table beside the sofa before he rose and placed the picture facedown.

Eleven

Two months later

"Monica?"

At the sound of her name being called, she turned in the lobby of her apartment building with her heart still pounding from discovering a few paparazzi following her while she was out shopping. News and rabid speculation on her and Gabe's breakup had forced them back into the public eye.

She gasped to see Phoebe rising from one of the ornate seats in the waiting area, looking pretty in coral wide-leg pants and a long-sleeved white tee. The sight of her and the obvious compassion in her eyes struck a chord in Monica as she let her shoulders slump and shook her head as emotions overwhelmed her. Phoebe gave her a smile and opened her arms wide, just as she'd promised that day in the attorney's office.

"Just know there is no deadline on when you reach out to me. Be it a day or a year or a dozen—if I'm still alive God willing—I will accept you with open arms."

In her, at that moment, Monica saw something she felt she'd never had before. Family. As she quickly crossed the divide and welcomed her aunt's embrace, she felt foolish for never fully allowing the woman into her life. "You came," she whispered, comforted by the warm pats on her back.

"You needed me," Phoebe said with a low chuckle. "Right?"

Monica nodded her head where it rested against her shoulder. "Right," she admitted.

"So here I am," Phoebe simply said.

Monica took a deep steadying breath before taking a small step back and looking at her aunt. "I love him," she admitted as tears welled.

Phoebe put a hand to her back. "Let's go up, have something to drink, and talk," she said.

"I don't have any juice or tea," Monica said as they reached the double doors of the elevators.

"Tea?" her aunt scoffed. "More like a mar-*ti*-ni."

That made Monica laugh. Maybe her first time in weeks.

As they settled in her living room and sipped on the dirty martinis Phoebe made for them, Monica felt comforted by the presence of this woman she really didn't know. "To have you here when I needed someone most makes me realize I wanted you here all along," she admitted.

Phoebe crossed her ankles and reached over to squeeze Monica's hand with hers. "When I saw the press about the breakup and saw the paparazzi hounding you again, I was determined to fly back and check on you," she said. "You looked so sad. I could see that."

"It's been two months, actually, so everyone's a little late," she said, thinking of the last time she'd seen Gabe. "Or someone is so overjoyed it's done, they gave the paparazzi a clue."

With each day her hope that he would come and fight for her faded. Still, she hungered for him. He was in her thoughts so often. It was like nothing she had ever experienced. Nothing at all. Her love for her ex seemed juvenile in comparison.

And it was then she realized that she loved Gabe.

His strength. His passion. His intelligence. His compassion. Even his drive and ambition.

Without her realizing it, Gabriel Cress had claimed a piece of her heart, and every day she had to deal with having that love without having him.

"I was a fool to think I could avoid loving him," Monica said, kicking off the heels she wore with her wrap dress and tucking her feet beneath her bottom as she looked out the window. "No, I was a fool to think I didn't already love him before that first wild night on the roof."

"The roof?" Phoebe said before fanning herself.

Monica felt her face flush with heat at the memory.

"Tell me the story of Monica and Gabe," Phoebe said.

In an instant she seemed to remember so many moments they'd shared. Good times. *Great* times.

"I will tell you our story, even though it doesn't end well, because the beginning and the middle were amazing," Monica admitted softly, feeling her pulse race.

At times she smiled. Other times her eyes glazed over as she remembered their heat. There were many moments she chuckled at something funny they'd shared together. And then, as she spoke of the weeks leading up to the night of her charity gala, she felt weighted down by her sadness. And regret.

"You *do* love him," Phoebe said with emphasis.

Monica looked to her.

"I see it in the way you talk about him, and remember him," the elder explained. "And miss him."

"But he broke my heart. He gave up. He walked away. He left me," Monica said, working her fingers as if to remove the tension she felt rise like a wave.

Phoebe stilled the frantic movement of her hand by covering it with her own. *"Or…"*

Monica looked to her again.

"Or your time together had come to its natural end," the older woman offered. "If you spend a chunk of your life with someone and the majority is good—truly good—then you should never end it hating the other person. You move on and keep the good memories, learn the life lessons and be prepared for your next big adventure."

"Another man?" Monica asked with a frown.

"No, not always. Sometimes you discover you in a way that you've never really known yourself. Or you travel. Or change careers. Or journal. Discover religion. Or write a book—and for some, hell, read a book. Or sometimes you discover you have a family member you never knew about and wished that you had," she said.

Monica's smile to her was warm and genuine.

"Life is all about change and newness, and sometimes people aren't meant to be in your life forever... and the time you spent together is nothing to regret, no matter how it ends."

"Like seasons?" Monica asked, rising to walk over to the window and look out at Central Park in the distance. The emerald green of the grass and the bright colors of the flowers gave it an idyllic look from where she stood.

"Exactly," Phoebe stressed. "Each just as necessary as the last. Some more brutal than others."

Monica crossed her arms over her chest. She blinked away tears that threatened to fall. She'd cried enough of them to fill a pond.

As she looked down at the street, she spotted a couple with their arms entwined as they walked and talked with each other. They laughed together before he wrapped an arm around her waist to lift her off her feet and spin her before pressing a kiss to her cheek. It was like a scene from a romance movie. It even seemed to move along in slow motion, but she knew that was her imagination at play.

How long will their season last? And how will it end? A fiery explosion or a gentle goodbye? Or will it last forever?

Gabe.

She thought of him as she had a million times over the last two months—especially at night when the world seemed quiet and there was no work at the foundation, lunch with friends or enough TV shows to keep her mind occupied. She focused on the good times they shared. Those happy, pleasure-filled memories eased her heartache. Not much. But some.

Maybe even enough to do something she thought she'd dare not.

Monica looked over her shoulder at the writing desk against the wall before she turned and walked over to it, then bent and removed a large envelope from the wastepaper basket. It was dark brown, like chocolate, with gold block letters. She licked her lips as she traced her name and address before touching that of GABRIEL. The restaurant—*his* restaurant. Not the man.

"He did it," she said, with the soft hint of a smile.

"Who?" Phoebe asked from the sofa.

Monica looked over at her as she held up the envelope between her index and middle finger. "It's an invite to his restaurant opening," she said. "It came earlier this week and I threw it away."

Phoebe kept her eyes locked on her niece but said nothing.

"I'm happy for him. I am," Monica stressed. "But I do not want to see him and the thing he chose over me. Ever. Am I wrong?"

Phoebe came over, gently took the envelope from her and set it on the center of the small modern-style desk next to a short stack of bills. "No, just undecided," she said.

True.

"When is it?"

"Next week," Monica said, digging her toes into the plush pile of the area rug. "Seems a little last-minute."

"Maybe he was undecided, too," Phoebe offered.

"Maybe," she said, wrinkling her brow a bit as she moved back to the window and stepped inside a ray of sunlight, which felt good against her skin.

Almost as good as Gabe.

Was he with someone new? Or was the restaurant his one true love?

"Well, you have a week to decide," Phoebe suggested from behind her.

Monica remained silent. Her thoughts were filled with visions of walking up on Gabe holding and kissing and giving attention to another woman the way he used to do with her. The jealousy she felt at just the idea of that was telling.

Her love for him lingered.

"What if his true intent was an invite to reconcile?" Phoebe asked.

Monica's heartbeat seemed to echo loudly inside her even as she shook her head in denial of the thought. "Hurt me once, shame on you. Hurt me twice?" she asked, using her own play on words of the popular saying. "Shame on me."

At the gentle nudge against her arm, she was surprised to find her aunt standing beside her with a fresh cocktail in each hand. She took one with a nod of thanks. "You make a really good drink, Auntie," she said after a long and satisfying sip.

"I was a bartender in this little dive in Cuba for two years when I was deeply in passion with Armando," Phoebe said as she lightly stroked her neck and smiled at some memory before sipping her drink, giving a soft little grunt from the back of her throat.

"Armando, huh?" Monica asked, curious about the life her aunt had lived that had included a stay in Cuba.

"Yes, and Frank, and Marcus, and Harry. Just to name a few," she said, her smile widening with each name. "I've had some great passions in my life. And I gave as good as I got."

"What about love?" she asked the older woman she was quickly learning to adore.

"Love? Sometimes," Phoebe said with a little shrug. "But even when the love fades the memories remain, and that, my niece, makes it *all* worthwhile."

With Gabe there had been more good than bad. So much more. Plenty of passion, laughs and deep conversations. Travels. Adventures. Discoveries. And the sex. Their physical connection. She shook her head in wonder at the thought of the heated moments they'd shared. The things they did to each other.

But…

"I'm too hurt to enjoy the memories," she admitted.

"Of course, you are…now," Phoebe assured her. "That's the good thing about memories, because they don't go anywhere. They'll wait for when you're ready to savor them, and they'll sneak up on you when you least expect it."

Don't I know it.

"To the memories," Phoebe said raising her glass with her eyes filled with twinkle.

Monica gave her a reluctant smile, anxious for the days her recollections didn't mock her so much. "To the memories," she agreed as they touched glasses.

Ding.

Gabe sprinkled thinly sliced green onions on the short ribs braised in red wine atop thick grits made savory with French Brillat-Savarin cheese and freshly made garlic butter. He stepped back to view his handiwork as he tossed his hand towel over his left shoulder and set his hands on his hips. "Run the dish," he said with a nod, signaling the plated meal was ready to be served.

It was the last dish of the first night of his restaurant's grand opening.

"Excellent job, Chef."

Gabe smiled as he extended a hand to Lorenzo, who had humbly served as his sous chef for one more night. Together they had effortlessly served those private guests he'd invited to celebrate with him. Tomorrow he would be on his own. GABRIEL was open. "Thank you, Chef."

"It's nice to see you smile, amigo," Lorenzo said as he walked over to the leather-covered double doors to remove his apron and free his shiny ebony waist-length hair.

This time the grin was forced. "I'm okay, Zo," he lied, moving to the wash sink to clean and dry his hands before replacing the dark brown, monogrammed chef's coat he wore with a clean one.

"You can't wake a person who is pretending to be asleep," Lorenzo said, pulling on a dark blue linen jacket that matched his dark denim jeans and deep blue silk shirt.

His friend had said the Navajo saying to him many times over the last two months. "I am moving on," he insisted.

"You're going through the motions," Lorenzo insisted. "Living without living."

He wasn't wrong. The nights were the worst.

"Call her, Gabe."

His gut felt punched at the very thought of her. He shook his head. "No," he said adamantly.

Lorenzo held up his hands. "Your life," he said.

"Yes, and a new part of it starts tonight," Gabe said, glad to move on from yet another what-went-wrong conversation.

"Yes, it does. Enjoy it," his friend said before turning and leaving him alone in the small but well-stocked kitchen.

Gabe released a short but deep breath as he nodded as if he were an athlete prepping himself on the sidelines before he entered a championship game. Success or failure rested on his shoulders because everything had been his selection from the small staff, the menu, the schematics and the interior design. Every bit of it was how he wanted to be viewed as a chef to the world. More than ever before.

His sacrifice had been great and he wanted the reward to surpass that.

He needed not to feel like the biggest fool ever.

He thought of a sweet moment with Monica, laughing at something he said as they lounged in bed, but forced the thought away.

Clearing his throat, Gabe pushed through the double doors and stepped out to the front of the house. The restaurant was small and intimate with a clean and stylish decor of pale walls, dark furnishings, and bronze votive candles and floral arrangements on each of the sixteen tables. Large quarter-top windows ran across the front of the space, showcasing the brick-lined street and the river in the distance. In the deep alcove on the side wall, he'd placed the bar, with its copper background and recessed lights illuminating the array of bottles lined up on the wood shelves. He would be open for four hours, six nights a week with a focus on dinner service, offering a delectable five-course tasting menu of his choosing. He would cook what he wanted and charge a premium price to do so, with a new menu printed every night. A new inspiration every night.

Never had he felt so inspired.

He stepped deeper into the restaurant, and the applause began. With a nod of thanks, Gabe looked about the room at all the smiling faces and felt comforted that his family was among them. For a moment, he wondered if their support was more about genuine desire for his success or because he had returned to Cress, INC. in a less prominent role while making it clear he was not interested in being the CEO upon their father's retirement. He could be there only if he was out of the race. He had begun to miss his family and the great work they were doing at Cress, INC. just as much as he'd craved being a chef again.

Stop being so dogged in your pursuit of success.

Mend the divide between you and your family.

Find a balance between what you want and what you need.

What he'd once felt was Monica's ultimatum or attempt to control his life had become some of the greatest advice he'd ever received. And when he'd reached out to his parents, it was with clear intent that it was his way or no way. Finally, he'd spoken up for himself and shed the desire to be unproblematic. Having them concede to him had been shocking and satisfying. They'd missed him, as well. For once he'd thought his father saw his worth. But in that moment, he'd felt even more gratified knowing he didn't *need* their approval or support.

Still it was nice to have—

The rest of his thoughts abruptly halted as he looked up and caught sight of Monica sitting at one of the tables near the windows. Surprise caused his heart to swell in his chest, and he felt a nervous energy course over his body as he took her in, feeling a hunger that was familiar. She wore more makeup than usual. Her smoky eyes, high cheekbones and nude glossy lips were beautiful. Her hair was pulled back from her face and behind her shoulders, framing large diamond chandelier earrings. But it was when she rose from the chair as he moved toward her that he truly felt out of breath.

The strapless black column dress was ruched at the middle, emphasizing her shape, with a hem that fell just below her knees, revealing well-toned legs and strappy heels with satin bows at the ankles.

She was stunning.

As he neared her, he saw the uncertainty in her eyes. He felt the same way.

"Hello, Monica," he said.

"Congratulations, Gabe," she said, her eyes unlocking with his to look beyond his shoulder for a moment.

He followed her line of vision to find his entire family looking at them. They all suddenly pretended to focus on their drinks and each other. Shaking his head, he looked back at her. "I can't believe you're here," he admitted, wondering if his pounding heart was as loud to her as it was to him.

"Thank you for the invite," she said.

Gabe didn't hide his confusion. "But I didn't send an invite," he admitted.

Monica frowned, then looked disappointed before her expression went blank. She looked down at her feet, then up at him. "Oh," she said before quickly turning and picking up her black-beaded clutch from the table.

"Gabe."

He looked over his shoulder to find his publicist, Frank Lawson, standing behind him.

"It's time for the toast," Frank said.

Gabe eyed two servers bringing trays of champagne-filled flutes from the bar. Just as planned. In attendance were a well-known food critic and a couple of mem-

bers of the press given exclusive access to the opening. "One moment," he said without a second thought.

Frank looked concerned. "I don't know if I can hold
them, Gabe," he said.

But he had already turned back to Monica, only
to find she was gone. The remembered look of disappointment in her eyes fueled him as he took the few
steps to yank open the copper-trimmed glass door to
step out onto the street. His heart wildly pounded as
he looked left and then right. She was nearing the corner to cross the street.

"Monica!" he called to her.

She stopped and turned.

The streetlamp above her highlighted the track of
a tear, like the twinkle of a star. A visceral pain radiated across his chest as he rushed to her.

"I shouldn't have come," she said, raising her hand
to her face.

Gabe covered it with his to lower it. He used his
free hand to capture the tear with his thumb as his eyes
moved over her face, taking in everything. His gaze
lingered on her mouth. "I'm glad you came," he admitted in a whisper. "You coming into my life in the first
place gave me the courage to do it all."

She closed her eyes and shook her head slowly as
she gripped his hand and slowly removed his touch.
"I came. I ate some really great food. I saw you. I said
my congrats. And now I'm leaving, Gabe."

"No, don't leave me," he pleaded, not allowing
shame or ego to make him act a fool again. "The worst

mistake I ever made was not fighting for us that night. Forgive me."

Monica gasped and then winced as she took a deep breath. "Gabe," she began.

"I thought you were angry at me. I thought you never wanted to see me again. I thought I hurt you so bad that I didn't have a right to convince you that I realized I love you," he said, holding tight to her hand and massaging tiny circles on the back of it as he enjoyed the simple physical connection. "*Forgive* me."

Monica kept her eyes closed as if it pained her to even look at him.

That hurt. But he understood it.

"Damn it," she swore as her shoulders slumped and she allowed her head to rest against his chest.

He rested his chin atop it. "*Forgive* me," he begged. "Gabe."

He heard Frank behind him but ignored him as he waited for Monica to honor his request. He wanted her back in his life more than everything, and he refused to give up the opportunity to fight for her for anything.

"I was a fool, baby, please," he stressed, easing back from her enough to press his hand to her face to raise it.

Her eyes remained closed.

"Look at me," he whispered.

Slowly, she did.

It was his turn to gasp as he looked into the brown depths of her eyes and saw every bit of the love she had for him. It was pure and real...and fierce. That he knew without her speaking. It was the epitome of wearing her heart on her sleeve.

Relief coursed over him until he felt strengthened and weakened all at once.

"Gabe!"

Monica leaned to the side to look past him. "They need you back at the restaurant," she said, as she looked back up at him.

"It can wait. Nothing matters to me more in this moment than you," he said steadfastly.

She looked at him again.

When her eyes widened in surprise, he turned, as well, to find his mother guiding Frank back inside the restaurant.

Gabe and Monica looked back at each other with questions in their eyes.

Did she send the invite?

"No," they said in unison before sharing a laugh that lightened the mood.

Monica dropped her head to his chest again and settled her hands on his hips. "Gabe, I have to be honest," she began.

He stiffened.

Is she with someone else?

The thought of that was torture.

"I learned some things these last couple of months," she said, raising her head to look up at him.

He enjoyed the sight of her. His eyes wandered over her as if he were feeding a hunger.

"About myself. About love. Family. So many things," Monica continued.

He'd felt anguish when he'd thought he had lost her forever.

"I *love* you, Gabriel Cress," she stressed, tilting her head to the side as her eyes searched his. "I forgive you."

So, this is joy.

"*If*—" she continued.

He tensed again, feeling completely shaken by the emotional roller coaster. His hint of a smile faded.

"*If* you can forgive me for letting my past filter everything you did and see it all in a bad light," she said, easing her hands around his waist. "*Forgive* me."

Gabe released the breath he hadn't realized he was holding. "Without question," he said, his voice deep and brimming with meaning as he brought his hands up under her hair to hold her neck and jaw in his palms.

They stared at each other. The energy—that familiar pulse—was there as their serious expressions were replaced with slow smiles. Long, endless moments of just enjoying being in one another's company again.

This was love.

Pure and profound.

He lowered his head, giving in to his hunger, and she tilted her head up and welcomed his kisses. Slow and soft at first, with moments in between each where their lips barely touched and they inhaled of one another's shaky breaths. And when they deepened, each moaned from down within as they clung to one another, until their bodies seemed to blend.

Gabriel knew in that moment that he loved her like he had never loved before, and that she had claimed a piece of his heart that no other woman would ever be able to reach. And there was not one bit of fear in him about it. Not one.

This was love.

Why had they denied themselves for so long?

It was Monica who broke the kiss and smiled at him as she cleaned her gloss from his lips with her thumb. She slid her hand in his. "You have an opening to attend," she reminded him.

"Let's walk slow," he said with a deliberate look down at the length of him hard and pressing against his pants.

She chuckled as she leaned against his arm. "My desire is not as easy to see," she said.

"The thought of that isn't helping," Gabe said, his voice deep.

"Maybe I should put a little distance between us," she said, slightly teasing as she released his hand.

"Not too much."

"Never again," she said, stopping as they came to the front door. She held up her pinky finger. "I promise not to ever push you away and you promise to never leave. Deal?"

Gabe hooked his pinky with hers. "Deal. No fear?"

"No fear," she agreed.

When they finally walked inside, the sounds of a successful restaurant surrounded them. Conversation blended with jazzy music. Forks hit dishes and glasses touched each other in toasts. Monica made a move to reclaim her seat, but Gabe held steadfastly to her hand to guide her behind him to the center of the restaurant where his family sat.

Frank looked relieved as he motioned for the servers to bring two additional flutes.

"What made you send the invite?" he heard Monica ask his mother.

"I was tired of seeing my son miserable without you," his mother replied.

So, it was her.

He cleared his throat and stared down at his feet to gather himself before he finally looked over at his mother. By sending that invite, she had accepted and welcomed Monica into the fold. For him.

That, too, was love.

Gabe accepted the flutes and handed one to Monica before facing his guests. "I'm proud and humbled to announce that GABRIEL has full reservations for the next four weeks. Thank you for the first of hopefully many nights to come of good food, good drink and good times. This is my life's dream, and I'm honored to share this night with all of you, with my family who taught me everything I know about food, and this woman beside me who taught me everything I know about love," he said, looking down at Monica, who was already looking at him.

The night was perfect.

"To GABRIEL," Phillip Sr. said.

As everyone in the restaurant raised their glasses in a toast to him and his establishment, Gabe looked over at his father and saw pride for him in his eyes. He had grown beyond needing his father's approval, but in truth, it was an honor to have. Extending his flute, he touched his glass to his father's before then lifting it into the circle created by his family with their own glasses raised in toast.

Atop the table, he covered Monica's hand with his own and entwined their fingers.

"À la nourriture. À la vie. À l'amour," he said, leveling his eyes on each of his family members.

"À la nourriture. À la vie. À l'amour," they all said in unison.

With his thumb still stroking the back of her hand, he leaned in close to her ear. "To food. To life. To love," he said before pressing a kiss behind her lobe.

He felt her tremble. "Soon," Gabe promised.

Monica looked at him, her soft eyes filling with heat. "Another wild night like the first one, Mr. Cress?" she said for his ears alone.

His pulse raced as he chuckled. "Better," he promised.

Epilogue

Three months later

"Marry me."

Monica opened her eyes and looked up at Gabe as he paused in delivering delicious stroke after stroke inside her. She lay beneath his strong, muscled frame in the center of their king-size bed. "You're doing this right now?" she asked in between deep gasps.

Gabe kissed both corners of her mouth. "Yes," he said before deepening the kiss with his clever tongue as he resumed stroking inside her, slowly. Deeply.

She released a tiny cry, feeling his hardness pressing against her walls. Her fingernails dug into his fleshy buttocks as she took the lead and suckled his tongue into her mouth, using her hips to meet his pace.

"Wait," he gasped, stopping all movement.

"What?" she asked, pressing her head back against the softness of the pillow to look up at him.

"Don't move. I'm not ready to come. Not yet," he said, resting his forehead against the pillow beside her as he clenched and unclenched his jaw, seeking control of his body.

She smiled as she worked the muscles of her intimacy to grip and release his hard inches slowly.

He tensed. "No, Monica," he pleaded, raising his head to look down at her.

"What?" she asked again, this time with feigned innocence.

He smiled before capturing her mouth with his. "I could stay inside you forever," he said.

"Really?" she asked as she rubbed the soft heel of her foot against his calf and stroked his nape with her fingertips.

"Absolutely."

She chuckled. "We wouldn't get much accomplished," she reminded him.

"Hell with the rest," he said.

She eyed him for long moments, amazed at how freely she accepted her love for him. Her trust of him. Her desire for it to last. And how much she believed he loved her just as deeply. "Monica Cress, huh?"

"Sounds good," he said, nuzzling her neck and kissing her racing pulse as he began to roll his hips to stroke his hardness inside her again.

"Monica Darby-Cress," she sighed as she arched her back and closed her eyes in pleasure.

"That's cool, too," Gabe said, raising his head to look down at her. "As long as I can call you my wife, the name change is up to you."

Monica struggled to stay focused on his words as his lovemaking wreaked havoc on her senses. The smell of him. The feel of his body and his sweat pressed down upon hers as he made love to her slowly, his hardness filling her and slickly striking against her bud. She opened her eyes to watch his profile as he opened his mouth against her shoulder and gasped in pleasure.

"Your wife," she said, wrapping her legs around him as she dug her fingers into his back.

Gabe looked at her. "My wife," he said, with a deep thrust that caused them both to gasp sharply.

She licked her lips, feeling parched from their explosive heat. "My husband," she whispered.

He fixed his wild eyes on hers. "Your husband," he said.

"Absolutely," she said, raising her head to capture his mouth with her own.

With a primal moan, he slipped his hands beneath her to cup her buttocks as he quickened his pace inside her. Swift. Deep. Thrilling.

Monica had been sucking his tongue but freed it as she cried out. Her release came in a rush and exploded deep inside her. She gave in to the pleasure and got lost in the madness. "Gabe!" she gasped as tears welled from the passion and her love for him.

He roared in that hot second just before she felt his rod get harder inside her as he filled her with his seed. Even in the midst of her passion, with her body still trembling, she rocked her hips back and forth, drawing everything from him and evoking even more primal moans and cries. She pushed through her own weakness, brought on by her climax, and relentlessly stroked downward on his hardness until he released one last, rough cry before his entire body went slack upon her.

"Damn," he swore. "Damn."

Monica pressed kisses from his neck to his shoulder, tasting the salt of his hard-earned sweat as she enjoyed the synchronized, fast tempo of their pounding heartbeats. "My love?" she said as she drew circles in the sweat on his back with her fingertip.

Gabe opened one eye. "Huh?" he asked, his oncoming sleep already deepening his voice further.

"Small and private wedding ceremony?" she suggested innocently, already thinking of the field day the press would have with anything else.

Gabe pressed a kiss to her shoulder, cheek and then mouth before rolling over onto his back. "Short engagement?" he countered.

Monica sat up to reach for the sheet from the floor to pull over their bodies before lying on her side and resting her head on his chest. "Honeymoon in Fiji?" she asked.

He fell quiet and she knew he was thinking of time away from the restaurant and Cress, INC.

"One week or two?"

She bit back a smile. "One," she said, knowing any time off would be hard for him to handle.

"Nah, two," he said.

She raised her head to look at him in surprise. "Two?" she said.

He chuckled as he stroked her hair back from her face. "It's my job to make you happy, future Mrs. Cress," he said.

She moved to staddle him and grabbed his hand to place them on her breasts. "Then round two, Mr. Cress?" she asked.

His eyes darkened with heat. "Your wish is always my command," he said with a roguish smile as she lowered her body so they could kiss and begin to give each other a *very* happy ending.

* * * * *

WE HOPE YOU ENJOYED
THIS BOOK FROM

*Luxury, scandal, desire—welcome to
the lives of the American elite.*

Be transported to the worlds of oil barons, family dynasties,
moguls and celebrities. Get ready for juicy plot twists,
delicious sensuality and intriguing scandal.

6 NEW BOOKS AVAILABLE EVERY MONTH!

SPECIAL EXCERPT FROM

◆ HARLEQUIN

DESIRE

When a scandal jeopardizes playboy CEO Drew Maddox's career, he proposes a fake engagement to his brilliant and philanthropic friend Jenna Sommers to revitalize his reputation and fund her efforts. But as passion takes over, can this bad boy reform his ways for her?

Read on for a sneak peek at
His Perfect Fake Engagement
by New York Times *bestselling author Shannon McKenna!*

Drew pulled her toward the big Mercedes SUV idling at the curb. "Here's your ride," he said. "We still on for tonight? I wouldn't blame you if you changed your mind. The paparazzi are a huge pain in the ass. Like a weather condition. Or a zombie horde."

"I'm still game," she said. "Let `em do their worst."

That got her a smile that touched off fireworks at every level of her consciousness.

For God's sake. Get a grip, girl.

"I'll pick you up for dinner at eight fifteen," he said. "Our reservation at Peccati di Gola is at eight forty-five."

"I'll be ready," she promised.

"Can I put my number into your phone, so you can text me your address?"

"Of course." She handed him her phone and waited as he tapped the number into it. He hit Call and waited for the ring.

"There," she said, taking her phone back. "You've got me now."

"Lucky me," he murmured. He glanced back at the photographers, still blocked by three security men at the door, still snapping photos. "You're no delicate flower, are you?"

"By no means," she assured him.

"I like that," he said. He'd already opened the car door for her, but as she was about to get inside, he pulled her swiftly back up again and covered her mouth with his.

His kiss was hotter than the last one. Deliberate, demanding. He pressed her closer, tasting her lips.

Oh. Wow. He tasted amazing. Like fire, like wind. Like sunlight on the ocean. She dug her fingers into the massive bulk of his shoulders, or tried to. He was so thick and solid. Her fingers slid helplessly over the fabric of his jacket. They could get no grip.

His lips parted hers. The tip of his tongue flicked against hers, coaxed her to open, to give herself up. To yield to him. His kiss promised infinite pleasure in return. It demanded surrender on a level so deep and primal, she responded instinctively.

She melted against him with a shudder of emotion that was absolutely unfaked.

Holy crap. Panic pierced her as she realized what was happening. He'd kissed her like he meant it, and she'd responded in the same way. As naturally as breathing.

She was so screwed.

Jenna pulled away, shaking. She felt like a mask had been pulled off. That he could see straight into the depths of her most private self.

And Drew helped her into the car and gave her a reassuring smile and a friendly wave as the car pulled away, like it was no big deal. As if he hadn't just tongue-kissed her passionately in front of a crowd of photographers and caused an inner earthquake.

Her lips were still glowing. They tingled from the contact.

She couldn't let her mind stray down this path. She was a means to an end.

It was Drew Maddox's nature to be seductive. He was probably that way with every woman he talked to. He probably couldn't help himself. Not even if he tried.

She had to keep that fact firmly in mind.

All. The. Time.

Don't miss what happens next in...
His Perfect Fake Engagement
by New York Times *bestselling author Shannon McKenna!*

Available March 2021 wherever
Harlequin Desire books and ebooks are sold.

Harlequin.com

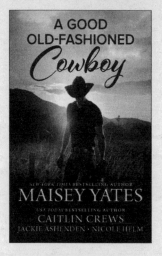